The
Scorpion's
Tail

The Doomsday Rats Book Two

The
Scorpion's
Tail

James Moloney

gus&Robertson
print of HarperCollins*Publishers*

Angus&Robertson
An imprint of HarperCollins*Publishers*

First published in 2005
by HarperCollins*Publishers* Pty Limited
ABN 36 009 913 517
A member of the HarperCollins*Publishers* (Australia) Pty Limited Group
www.harpercollins.com.au

HarperCollins*Publishers*
25 Ryde Road, Pymble, Sydney NSW 2073, Australia
31 View Road, Glenfield, Auckland 10, New Zealand
77–85 Fulham Palace Road, London W6 8JB, United Kingdom
2 Bloor Street East, 20th floor, Toronto, Ontario M4W 1A8, Canada
10 East 53rd Street, New York NY 10022, USA

National Library of Australia Cataloguing-in-Publication data:

Moloney, James, 1954–.
    The scorpion's tail.
    For children aged 9–13 years.
    ISBN 0 2071 9666 4.
    I. Title. (Series: Moloney, James, 1954– Doomsday Rats
    series; bk.2).
A823.3

Cover illustration by Marc McBride
Series design by Darian Causby, Highway 51 Design Works
Internal design by HarperCollins Design Studio
Typeset in Bembo 13.5/18pt by Helen Beard, ECJ Australia Pty Ltd
Printed and bound in Australia by Griffin Press on 60gsm Bulky Paperback

5 4 3 2 1   05 06 07 08

FOR HENRY, LILY, CLOE
AND TOM

CONTENTS

ONE They Know We are Down Here 1

TWO Deadly Crossbow 11

THREE The Probe 21

FOUR The Creature Must Die 34

FIVE Mission to the Surface 42

SIX To Kill in Cold Blood 53

SEVEN Blackout 61

EIGHT A New and Deadly Foe 71

NINE A Gift for a Saviour 80

TEN The Scorpion Returns 89

ELEVEN Sector Nine 99

TWELVE Battle by Sonar 109

THIRTEEN The Scorpion's Tail 120

FOURTEEN A Trickle of Water 130

FIFTEEN Darkness and Death 140

SIXTEEN A Choice of Targets 149

ONE

They Know We are Down Here

BERRIN'S SWORD SCRAPED noisily against the concrete as he crawled through the narrow tunnel. He was a slim boy, some would say skinny, but if this helped him get around inside the storm-water pipes that had become his home, then he didn't care what people called him. He tilted his head a little so that the lamp attached to his helmet could punch through the darkness in front of him. He caught just a glimpse of a figure crawling ahead of him. Come on, better keep up, he told himself. They'll be waiting for me.

He crouched lower to keep the handle of his sword away from the tunnel's hard shell. This was the new sword he had been given to replace the one he had lost only hours before. Half a metre of razor-sharp steel, it was sheathed in a leather scabbard and strapped to his back. He would have to pull it free soon enough, he suspected. There would be fighting. He could already feel the fear twisting his stomach into a painful knot.

A few metres ahead, the pipe opened into a much larger one. He stood up at last and brushed the dirt from his hands. Human beings weren't made for crawling around inside tunnels like these. They weren't supposed to be hunted by cruel beasts called Gadges either. Half man, half wolf, the Gadges prowled the city streets above the storm-water drains. Berrin was one of only a handful of children who held out against them. They called themselves the Rats.

Here in this larger pipe, a light bulb spilled gloomy yellow light onto the young bodies. Like the others before him, Berrin quickly reached up to switch off his helmet lamp. Battery power was too precious to waste. The Rats were a ragged bunch. The shoulders and knees of their clothing had been worn away from the constant scraping against unfriendly concrete, and any colour had long since been lost under the grime. With little chance to see the sun, their skins would have been a deathly white, if not for the dirt.

The children had barely had time to stretch or turn to a friend for a comforting word when a boy named Ruben brought the news they had been dreading. 'They're coming. The Gadges are in the tunnels,' he gasped.

'Where? How many?' These blunt questions came from their leader, Dorian. She was older than the others, though not so old she couldn't fit inside the narrower tunnels. Her firm, commanding voice helped to calm their fears.

'All over. I don't know how many. They've come from different directions, I'm sure of that,' Ruben answered solemnly. He didn't like being the messenger who had brought such terrible news. 'Maybe they still don't realise we live down here,' he went on. 'Maybe they think Berrin and the others used the pipes this morning to escape to somewhere else. They could be just waiting for them to come out.'

Only hours before, Berrin had made a fateful decision. Surrounded by Gadges who were ready to kill them, he had led his companions into the safety of the tunnels below ground. But in doing so, he had let the Gadges see them enter the storm-water drains. The precious secret had been revealed.

'Don't fool yourself,' said a deeper voice. 'They know we're down here.' This was Wendell, who had saved Berrin's life and brought him into the tunnels to become a Rat. Judging from the way he was looking at Berrin at that moment, he seemed to regret it.

Berrin's stomach churned miserably. He sensed a movement near his feet and found Jasper there, waiting to be picked up. Grey from head to toe, except for an odd tuft of white fur on his forehead, Jasper was a real rat. 'At least you won't give me a hard time,' he whispered to the rodent as he settled him gently on his shoulder.

'Wendell is right,' said Dorian. 'They know. Our days of hiding are over. We'll have to fight for these tunnels now.' She thought for a little longer. 'Most of all, we have to keep them away from here.'

No-one argued with her. The tunnels close by had become their base within the maze of so many pipes that drained the city above them. Electrical wires had been run down from the surface to give them light and to recharge their batteries. Each of the Rats had a comfortable hammock for sleeping above the dirt and, worse, the water that often flowed through the pipes. Their weapons were kept here and what little food they been able to store away. But more important than any of these reasons, one thought taunted them all. They had to keep the Gadges away from Ferdinand, their founder, who couldn't move about the tunnels like the rest of them.

'I'll stop them coming too close,' said Wendell.

'Me too,' Berrin volunteered just as quickly. He had a special reason for protecting their founder that none of the others shared. Ferdinand was his uncle.

'If you try to fight them hand to hand, they'll kill you,' said Dorian, as though she was talking about what to eat for dinner. 'We have to be clever about this. We know these tunnels and they don't. We can use our advantage to lure them away instead.'

Berrin was well ahead of her. He was already planning a strategy in his head. 'I'll need a Dodgem,' he announced.

'Take whatever you need.'

'You'll need me,' said a girl who stepped forward eagerly. It was Berrin's friend Olanda. Finely braided hair escaped from beneath her helmet and danced about her shoulders as she stretched and limbered up. Olanda was always ready, whether it was for a fight or an argument. Anything rather than stand still and be quiet.

Across the chamber, another Rat prepared to join them. It was Quinn, the worst Dodgem driver in the tunnels but the best shot with a crossbow. 'I'm with you, Wendell,' he called.

Two brave teams. Two Dodgems. Seconds later, they were on the move.

Dodgems were an ingenious creation of Ferdinand. With a steel frame and small black wheels powered by a heavy, rechargeable battery, they could scoot along the tunnels at a dazzling speed.

Quinn and Wendell had theirs moving first and so they took the lead. Wendell was too big for the seat, but this was no time to remind him. He crammed himself into the tight space, leaving the driving to Quinn. It was a decision Wendell soon regretted. Berrin and Olanda could see him swaying precariously in the seat behind his partner. 'I'd rather fight a Gadge than let Quinn drive me around in these tunnels,' Olanda called to Berrin.

After ten minutes of reckless cornering and breakneck speed, Quinn came to a halt. 'How far in do you think the Gadges have come?'

'Don't know,' Wendell grunted. 'Best thing is to wait here until they reach us.' Berrin and Olanda quickly joined them. 'Rig the Dodgems to run the other way then kill the light. We don't want to give them any warning,' Wendell ordered.

Moments later, Berrin gasped. There was no darkness like the pitch black that enveloped them when the lamps were turned off. 'Where will we lead them?' he asked the companions he could no longer see.

'Anywhere, so long as it's away from Ferdinand,' Wendell answered. He slid the sword from the scabbard tied to his back and felt the edge. 'Needs sharpening,' he commented.

They waited. There would be a light first, they guessed. That would be the signal. Once the Gadges picked them up with their torches, the chase would be on. None of them knew quite what to expect.

The minutes passed.

'Berrin,' Olanda called softly, for even she had learned to keep her voice down in the tunnels. 'Do you think Ferdinand is right? Will it soon be Doomsday for Malig Tumora?'

'You've forgotten how he said it,' Berrin told her gravely. 'It could just as easily be the end for us instead.'

His mind went back to the meeting that had finished not long before. Ferdinand was a grown-up, the only one in the city whom Malig Tumora did not control. His lanky body was frail and his skin so white that Berrin had thought he was a ghost at first. In a way he was, because his body was trapped underground.

Before Berrin had entered the tunnels, he had known nothing of families, of aunts and uncles, or even that he had a mother and father. He had lived in a cheerless dormitory with hundreds of children like himself. Their guardians were Dfx*, grim-faced creatures with just enough human being in them to raise the children as Malig Tumora wanted. When the children grew too old for the dormitories, they became slaves of this one man.

'We have to break Malig Tumora's control over the other adults before he destroys us,' whispered Berrin. 'At least we know what to do now.'

'The glasshouses,' said Olanda.

Berrin himself had discovered the huge buildings made of glass. Inside, he had found row upon row of purple flowers, as far as he could see. The fragrance of those flowers was a sweet trap. It left a human being helpless, with no will power at all. That was how Malig Tumora controlled the grown-ups.

'Yes, the glasshouses,' he replied. 'That's what we have to do now. Destroy them and free the grown-ups.'

Was that a noise? A footstep perhaps, the crush of gravel under a cruel paw. But sound could travel a long way in the tunnels. They had to keep their nerve.

* Dfx is pronounced 'Dee-fex'. The word is both singular and plural.

There, a second noise, more the rhythm of breathing this time. Still there was no glow against the tunnel walls. They needed to wait for the torchlight.

When the sound grew even louder, Berrin acted. It wasn't that fear had broken him down. They were all afraid. No, in that instant he had realised they might be making a simple but deadly mistake. They had assumed the Gadges would bring torches to light their way.

He flicked on his helmet lamp. From only twenty metres away, three Gadges stared at them. For a moment, the light from Berrin's helmet reflected in the perfect circles at the centre of their eyes.

Then they charged.

TWO
Deadly Crossbow

THE GADGES WERE MERCILESS creatures who could walk on their hind legs, like a man. In the tunnels, though, the largest ones were too big to walk upright. These three ran like wolves, their vicious snouts jutting forward, teeth bared.

Berrin dived into the seat of his Dodgem, desperate to be on the move. Olanda was just as quick. She landed in the driver's seat and, as soon as they were both aboard, rammed the control lever forward as far as it would go.

Just as well. Quinn had the other Dodgem moving and if they hadn't lurched forward when they did, he would have slammed into them.

'Faster!' Quinn shouted ahead to Olanda.

Behind him, Wendell had drawn his sword to poke awkwardly at the leading Gadge as he closed to within a metre. 'Careful!' Quinn shouted. If Wendell swung his sword too vigorously, he would tip them over and the Gadges would rip them to pieces before they could crawl out of the wreckage.

Wendell managed to nick the Gadge on the tip of its nose, bringing a brief yelp of pain. The growling beast fell back for a moment, giving them the space they needed. The Dodgems didn't fail them. Gradually, they were pulling away. The trouble was, they were leading the Gadges towards Ferdinand and that was the last thing they wanted.

'Go left at the next junction,' Berrin called to Olanda.

This was easy because the pipes parted in a narrow Y. As they entered the new tunnel, he turned round in his seat. Yes, Quinn had steered to the right, taking one of the Gadges with him. He would lead that one a merry dance away from their trapped leader. It was up to Olanda and Berrin to do the same with the two that still chased them.

'There's another junction coming up. Go left again.'

'It's a pretty sharp turn,' Olanda called back. 'I'll have to slow down.'

Berrin glanced over his shoulder and gasped at what he saw. 'No, don't slow down! Don't slow down!'

'Well, make up your mind, Berrin. Do you want to be killed by the Gadges or my driving?'

It didn't seem like much of a choice. And here was the junction emerging rapidly out of the darkness ahead.

Despite Berrin's plea, Olanda eased back on the lever and the Dodgem lost speed. The Gadges bounded closer.

Berrin pulled his sword free, ready to lash out, but he knew what those vicious jaws could do. One snap and he wouldn't just lose his sword, he'd lose his whole arm as well.

'Lean!' Olanda shouted.

'What?'

'Lean out to the left, as far as you can go.'

With his sword in one hand, Berrin clamped his other to the frame of the Dodgem and pushed as much of his body as he dared out to the left. At that instant, they lurched into the corner and Olanda slammed the lever forward again.

The wheels on the left side rose off the concrete. Would they tip over? They balanced precariously on two wheels for what seemed like a lifetime. Then, *bang*. They were back on all four wheels again and the Gadges were left in their wake.

'Where does this take us?' Olanda called.

'Sector Nine, I think. Dorian told us not to come up this way, remember.'

'Because of the Gunge?' she asked, referring to the blood-red plant that had tried to kill Berrin once already.

'I suppose. But didn't she mention something else? A Firedrake, that was it.'

'Oh, great! Gadges, Gunge and a Firedrake, whatever that is. Now it's my turn to choose my own death!' Olanda complained. Despite their fears, she managed a laugh. That was Olanda.

At yet another junction she slowed almost to a stop.

'What are you doing?' Berrin cried.

'We don't want to lose them just yet.'

She was right. Their job was to lead the Gadges away, to where they couldn't do any harm. As soon as Berrin's helmet lamp picked out the intruders, they set off again. But inside his head, Berrin could hear Dorian's warning. He wished he knew what a Firedrake was.

When they had drawn well ahead of the Gadges again, he called out to Olanda. 'This is far enough. Look for a side tunnel.'

This time, they had to slow down to a crawl. The Dodgem would fit inside the narrower tunnel but the turn could be tricky.

'There's one,' he said, pointing over Olanda's shoulder.

She brought them almost completely to a halt before turning. Then they were inside and she could speed up again. Instead, she stopped altogether.

'Come on, get moving.'

'There's nowhere to go,' she answered quickly.

'What?'

'See for yourself. This pipe branches into smaller ones just ahead.'

'Back up then. We'll have to find another one.'

To do this, they needed to turn around in their seats and change the light from one end to the other. They worked quickly, or at least they tried to, but the bracket that held the headlight in place was bent, making the light difficult to free. Every second was precious, and by the time they had the light off one end and onto the other, they had used up too many.

'We'll have to stay here and hope they go past,' Berrin whispered, killing the light.

They waited in the darkness. Less than a minute later, heavy panting filled the larger tunnel.

'Hold up,' panted a weary voice.

'We'll never catch them if you have to rest all the time,' complained his companion. They had stopped only a few metres past the opening where Berrin and Olanda waited anxiously.

The first Gadge took a deep gulp of air and swallowed hard. 'I'm not sure I do want to catch them.'

'What are you saying? That was the order from Gadger Red. Get them all, or chase them out into the open.'

'Yes, and because he's in such a hurry he's sent us into these wretched tunnels without lights or guns. Use what Malig Tumora gave you, he says. Your nose, your teeth, your claws. Well, I don't like it. Those little renegades have got it all their own way down here.'

His companion snorted in reluctant agreement.

Listening in the nearby pipe, Berrin almost did the same. Gadges were large creatures. When they stood upright, toting a gun like they did on the surface, they were awesome, enough to turn your mouth into a desert just looking at them. But here in the tunnels, they needed all their limbs for walking. He hadn't realised during the panic of their escape, but now the Gadges had told him themselves: they had no weapons. Well, none except their teeth and their claws, although these alone meant they were still a fearsome enemy. And Gadger Red had been right about one thing, as Berrin and Olanda were about to find out.

'Do you smell anything?' the first Gadge asked.

'Just the putrid stink of your sweat,' came the reply.

The insult was ignored. 'No, take a sniff,' the first insisted.

Berrin's skin went cold as he heard a deliberate intake of breath.

'I can smell those young humans, now that you mention it,' he said. 'But we know they came this way.'

'It's stronger than that,' said the first and Berrin knew then that they were going to be discovered. Already, the crunch of tiny stones under their paws told him they were moving about, sniffing, searching, their noses making up for what their eyes couldn't see.

'I can feel an opening off to the side. The smell's coming from here.'

Berrin held his sword ready, but he had another weapon that would be more effective, for a few seconds at least. When he felt their warm, fetid breath seeping into the narrow tunnel, he flicked on the Dodgem's headlight.

'Argh!' screamed one of the Gadges and threw his paws up to his face. Berrin darted forward and jabbed at his arm with the sword, bringing another cry of pain.

The second Gadge pushed his companion aside. Shielding his eyes with one paw, he leaned deep into the pipe, slashing and clawing at Berrin. The sword parried these first attacks and Berrin used the frame of the Dodgem to avoid the next, but it was only a matter of time before a razor-sharp claw sliced into his flesh.

'Duck!' Olanda shouted with such authority that he obeyed immediately. Something zinged only a hand's width above his skull and then a far louder cry of agony filled the tunnels. Berrin looked up to see the bolt from a crossbow buried in the Gadge's shoulder.

The loathsome beast's cry became the desolate howl of a wolf and he pulled back from the children.

'I've got more bolts ready if you come at us again,' Olanda warned them.

The Gadges were furious, but they made no more attacks. In such a narrow space, that crossbow could be deadly and they knew it.

As the wounded Gadge moaned in pain, the other growled out of the darkness, 'We're not finished with you. We'll be back and your crossbows and your swords won't help you then.'

More groaning and the irregular pad of paws along the tunnel told of their retreat. Berrin waited, straining his ears, but he knew it was no trick. Only fools fought on in the dark and without weapons. Gadges were no fools. They *would* be back, just as these two had promised.

When the creatures were long gone, Berrin and Olanda eased the Dodgem out of the narrow pipe. They were about to climb into their seats when a faint rumbling noise echoed along the tunnel. For an instant, a pale glow reflected against the curved walls and then died.

'What was that?' Berrin asked.

'Don't know, but it came from up that way.' Olanda pointed towards the forbidden zone, the area Dorian had called Sector Nine. 'Sounds alive,' she added, but since they were about to leave, in the opposite direction, she didn't seem in a hurry to find out more.

Berrin climbed into his seat behind her, hoping that he never found out either.

THREE
The Probe

BERRIN AND OLANDA RETURNED to base and found Wendell and Quinn already there.

'They didn't stand a chance,' Quinn was boasting. 'I put a bolt into one of them from behind.'

'Did you kill it?' Dorian asked.

'No, but there's one Gadge who won't be sitting down for a while. Should have heard him howl.'

They laughed, all except Dorian. 'Next time, aim at his heart, not his butt,' she said coldly.

Then she made Berrin and Olanda tell their story. 'Um,' she sighed as she scratched her elbow.

'Two Gadges wounded and the rest have run off with their tails between their legs. Gadger Red will have steam coming out of his ears.'

'It was his fault, though. He sent them in unprepared.' Berrin repeated the conversation he had overheard between the Gadges.

'Yes, he was too eager to get at us. You can bet he won't make the same mistake again,' added Dorian.

No-one argued with her ominous prediction.

It was late. On the surface, the sun would already be gone. Not that it made much difference down in the tunnels. But the Rats were exhausted and in need of sleep.

'Make sure the Dodgems are plugged into the recharger,' Dorian ordered wearily. 'And everyone will need new batteries for their helmet lamps.'

Scouts were sent out to watch the tunnels through the night. The rest of the Doomsday Rats fell into their hammocks.

Before he drifted into sleep, Berrin heard Olanda whisper to Dorian. It was something about Sector Nine. He listened in.

'So you heard it then?' Dorian was saying.

'I think so,' answered Olanda. 'But we didn't see it. Why is it called a Firedrake?'

'That was Ferdinand's name for it. He says it can breathe fire.'

'Breathe fire!' Berrin interrupted, forcing back a laugh. 'That's crazy. How can an animal breathe fire? Have you ever seen this Firedrake?'

'No,' Dorian replied.

'Then I don't believe there's any such thing.'

'Suit yourself,' said Dorian calmly, and moments later she was asleep.

IN THE MORNING, THEY gathered again beneath the light bulb to eat. They stole their food from the surface, wherever they could get it. There was a large bakery run by Dfx a kilometre away and, years before, the Rats had found a way in through an access hole in the basement. They were careful to steal only a few loaves at a time and if the slow-witted Dfx ever noticed a loaf or two missing, they probably blamed each other.

'With Gadges roaming around in our tunnels, how will we get more bread?' someone asked.

Dorian had no answer. She looked up at the light bulb and the precious glow it gave off. It wasn't just bread they couldn't do without, she realised with a shudder.

Berrin was devouring his last morsel when the dull hum of a Dodgem filled the tunnel. Moments later, Ruben brought it to a halt close by. 'Help me,' he called. 'Vindy's been wounded.'

They lifted the bony frame of a young girl carefully from the rear seat. Blood dripped onto the concrete but the wound wasn't serious.

'They're back and this time they've brought their guns with them,' Ruben explained.

'But they need their front legs to walk in the tunnels. How can they carry guns?' Berrin asked.

'Strapped to their backs, like we carry our swords. That's how we managed to get away. A Gadge surprised us, but it took him a few seconds to sit back on his haunches and grab for the gun.' Ruben looked miserably towards Vindy. 'We just had time to turn into a side tunnel, but he got off a shot before we were safe.'

'How could he see you?'

'They've got lights like ours, on top of their heads.'

'We've lost our advantage then,' said Wendell.

'Only in the largest tunnels,' Dorian pointed

out quickly. 'Gadges are too big for the smaller pipes. We'll have to stick to those now.'

'But that's not much use. The smaller pipes don't go very far. They keep joining up with the big ones.'

'It's the best we can do for now,' Dorian said. 'If we're going to survive at all, we have to drive them out. We'll surprise them with hit-and-run attacks like yesterday. Then escape into the smaller pipes where they can't reach us.'

It was a desperate plan. Dorian's face creased into a frown as she gave the orders and Berrin guessed it wasn't just the risks she was asking them all to take that disturbed her. 'What's the matter?' he asked softly, so that no-one else would hear.

Dorian turned to him, her eyes dull with worry. 'We're fighting just to stay alive now,' she whispered. 'While this takes up all our time, we can't send any missions to the surface to destroy the glasshouses. Malig Tumora is winning the war, even though he hasn't killed a single one of us.'

Berrin kept these fears to himself, as Dorian would have wanted. He didn't even mention them to Olanda when they set out together on foot soon afterwards. The Gadges hadn't come anywhere near the base yet, so they could afford to walk upright in the largest pipes. But after only a few minutes, they obeyed Dorian's command and crawled into a smaller one. Progress was slow and the pipes didn't always take them where they wanted to go. To make the journey even more difficult, water began to trickle along the bottom of the pipe.

'Rain,' said Berrin. He had known in the back of his mind that it would surely rain soon, up there on the surface, and when it did, they could expect this steady flow throughout the system. Now it had happened.

'Ugh, mud,' sighed Olanda, flicking the thick ooze from her hands.

Some of it landed on Berrin. 'Hey, watch out,' he complained. If there had been no Gadges roaming the larger tunnels, he might have flicked mud right back at her. There was nothing like a good mud fight for a bit of fun.

Jasper, the little rodent, had come with them, running ahead in the light from Berrin's lamp. Now that the bottom of the pipe had become an icy river of mud, he climbed Berrin's arm and perched himself between the boy's shoulder blades. 'Some scout, you are,' sniffed Berrin.

The water had disturbed other inhabitants of the darkened tunnels. Beetles and cockroaches climbed the walls. The Rats were used to the sight of them, but one creature demanded more caution.

'Watch out for the scorpion,' Olanda called back to Berrin. She crawled on, staying as far to the left as she could manage.

Berrin followed and quickly spotted the danger. 'It's more scared of us,' he commented when he saw the finger-length scorpion back away. Its tail was poised to defend itself. A scorpion sting could be very painful.

They crawled on, dreading the deadly task ahead. The tactic was simple. In teams of two, the Rats were to hide in the narrow side pipes, listening for the Gadges. Once the creatures had passed, the pair would slip out silently behind them. Then, one of them would flick on a helmet light while the other shot a bolt from the crossbow. There wouldn't even be time to see if the bolt had found its mark.

Instantly, the pair would have to throw themselves back into the side tunnel where the Gadges couldn't follow.

Simple! But one mistake, or just a few seconds of hesitation, and they were dead.

Berrin rehearsed each movement in his head. 'Our only advantage is that they don't know where we are hiding,' he whispered to Olanda.

He was about to discover that this last advantage had been stolen from them and in a way he could never have imagined.

THEY WORKED THEIR WAY slowly through the smaller pipes until they found one of the large tunnels ahead.

'Back up a little,' said Olanda, who was leading.

Berrin shuffled backwards.

'Here will do,' she whispered. 'We can't see the opening but we can hear if Gadges come by.'

Berrin felt his mouth go dry. He could think through what they had to do a hundred times, but that was different from the real thing.

They waited in darkness. With water flowing slowly between their hands and knees, they couldn't lie down. If they had to wait much longer they'd get cramps.

Then came the noise they had been waiting for, the noise they dreaded. Not just footsteps this time, but voices. Not just any voice either. It was Gadger Red himself.

'Bring her along,' he snarled.

Had they caught one of the Rats? A girl! Dorian herself, perhaps.

'She won't come any faster,' replied one of Gadger Red's companions. 'Look at her. She's not exactly built for speed.'

'I'm so sorry. This is as fast as I can go,' said a female voice. The gentle tones sounded strange amid the gruffness of the Gadges.

A faint light brushed the curve of the pipe where Berrin and Olanda were hiding. With a slight bend between them and the larger tunnel, they could not be seen. They could hear, though, as Olanda had predicted. When the crush of gravel underfoot ceased, they knew the party had stopped by the opening into their pipe.

This wasn't what they needed. No, not at all.

Keep going, Berrin pleaded with them silently. Just a little further. Then they could dare their attack. Perhaps they would kill Gadger Red himself. It was worth the risk. But the slow-moving female, whoever she was, needed a rest.

'What can you tell me, probe?' Gadger Red demanded.

'That the young humans have been along this tunnel.'

'My own nose can tell me that much,' Gadger Red snarled dismissively.

'Can your nose tell you there were two of them, in some kind of machine? Battery-powered. I smell nickel and cadmium. It's a rechargeable battery, I'd say. They came by yesterday, late in the afternoon. No-one has been here since.'

'That's better. Where's that machine now?'

'Let me touch the wall,' the gentle voice requested. A few moments of silence followed.

'Well?' Gadger Red asked impatiently.

'It's not moving at the moment. Not that one, anyway. There's one like it travelling very quickly, about two kilometres away. Not in this tunnel, though. Someone named Quinn is driving it. The passenger just shouted at him to slow down.'

'Can you pick up the rest of the children? A crowd of them, maybe. I want to know where they gather, where they sleep, where they store their supplies.'

This time, the soft female voice took even longer to respond. For Berrin, the silence stretched out unbearably. How did she do it? What kind of Gadge could hear voices from two kilometres away? Was it a Gadge at all, he wondered. Worst of all, would she pinpoint their base, even from this distance?

'Well, probe, have you found a group of them?' Gadger Red asked eagerly.

'No, they are not all in one place, Mr Gadger. I cannot say there is any one spot just yet.'

'But you can hear them?'

'Oh yes. Many of them. Some are quite close. There are two very near to us now, in fact. I can pick out their heartbeats. Very fast heartbeats. They must be rather frightened. There is something else with them. A small animal. From the smell, I'd say it's a rat.'

'How close? Where are they?'

'Down that pipe there,' said the soft voice, as though she was pointing out a pretty bunch of flowers.

Berrin and Olanda had heard every word. It was the mention of Jasper that galvanised them into action. They had been betrayed and there was no reason to stay still and silent any longer. Berrin grasped Olanda's ankle. 'Back up,' he hissed. 'Quickly.'

Already, he was crawling backwards as fast as he could manage. Olanda was just as desperate. Her filthy feet smacked into his face but he didn't stop to complain.

Then the firing started. The noise was deafening, but it wasn't the noise that worried them. If the pipe had been straight, they would have died there, one behind the other. But even the bend in the pipe couldn't save them entirely. Bullets glanced off the curved concrete and whizzed by their ears. Only when they had backed away forty metres were they safe.

But for how long? The Gadges couldn't follow them into this pipe, but did they need to? For all that she spoke with a gentle voice, that strange creature might prove more deadly than any Gadge. Somehow, she could see into the maze of pipes and pick out where the Rats moved and what they were saying.

Gadger Red wanted her to locate their base. For the moment she had failed, but if he took her deeper into the tunnels, it was only a matter of time.

FOUR

The Creature Must Die

'WE HAVE TO TELL DORIAN,' said Olanda as soon as the firing stopped.

Berrin grimaced and held his finger to his lips.

Olanda's almond-shaped eyes went round in horror as she realised. She put her hand over her mouth, though it was too late now. That strange creature they called a probe would have already heard her speak.

Berrin shocked her a second time when he began to scrape his sword across the hard concrete that surrounded them. It was so deliberate, so loud. The creature would surely hear that! But then he leaned close and whispered into her ear. 'She knows where we are anyway. The important thing is that she doesn't hear what we say.'

Olanda understood immediately and, drawing her sword, doubled the scraping sounds that masked their voices. 'How can we warn Dorian?'

'We'll have to get back to base as quickly as possible.'

'But Gadger Red will be expecting that. His creature will work out where we've gone. We'll end up leading them straight there.'

Berrin hadn't thought of that. He fell silent, stumped for the moment. Meanwhile, Olanda kept up the harsh scraping of her sword across the pipe's surface.

'Why don't I distract them?' she said. 'Get them chasing me. That creature won't be able to track you through the pipes then.'

'But it's way too dangerous on your own.'

'I'll join up with other Rats,' she assured him.

Further down the pipes, when they reached a junction, she moved off without him. He wanted to call out, to warn her. *Don't take any risks.* He didn't, though. Not because the strange creature would hear him, but because it was a stupid thing to say. Whether they liked it or not, their whole lives had already become one huge risk.

Berrin deliberately headed away from the base to start with. He had been moving for only a few minutes when a burst of gunfire echoed through the tunnels. 'Olanda!' he whispered and cursed himself for letting her go like that.

Faster than he had intended, he turned towards the base. More gunfire. It was faint, but what did that matter? To the Rats they were shooting at, it would sound like thunder.

At last he found the tunnel that led into the sleeping chamber. The only light came from his own helmet, but Dorian was there among the hammocks. Wendell, too. Their faces were a mirror of his own desolation.

'Where's Olanda?' was Dorian's first question.

Should he admit it? He had abandoned her and now she might be dead. Berrin pushed back his fears and left the question unanswered. 'The Gadges have brought a strange animal with them. They call it a probe. It could feel us breathing in the pipes nearby. It even heard Quinn's name being called from two kilometres away.'

'Me?' called a voice from the tunnel. Quinn appeared, followed closely by another pair of Rats who had just returned in a Dodgem.

'Have you seen Olanda?' Berrin asked anxiously.

All three shook their heads. 'I saw some blood on the wall of a pipe,' one said.

This was hardly the news Berrin had asked for.

Dorian wouldn't let herself be distracted by talk of blood. She considered what Berrin had told her.

Wendell didn't need as much time to decide. 'It's obvious what we have to do, isn't it?' he urged. 'We have to kill this probe creature before it leads them here.'

Berrin felt his heart lurch inside his chest. Kill it. Yes, they must, and quickly. Right now, the probe was more dangerous than Gadger Red himself. But at the same time, he could hear that gentle voice in his ears. Unlike Wendell and the others, he couldn't think of the creature as simply 'it'. In his mind, he used the word 'she'.

There was another word that seemed to attach itself to her, like mud that wouldn't wash away.

Innocent. The way she spoke so respectfully to the despicable Gadges almost made him laugh. And she had seemed so eager to please, without any thought for what the Gadges would do when they caught up with their quarry.

Dorian spoke at last. 'I agree with Wendell. If a creature can pick up so much just from the vibrations of the pipes, it will have the Gadges here in no time. It has to die.'

'But how?' Berrin demanded. 'Gadger Red is guarding her and there are at least two others with him. They have guns.'

He saw the crossbow in Quinn's hands. It seemed a poor weapon now, in the face of such frightening power. Nodding towards it, he went on, 'There would barely be time to fire a single bolt before they mowed us down.'

'You're right,' said Dorian and she took the crossbow from Quinn. When she spoke again, there was an odd tone of resignation in her voice. 'I'll only get one shot before they kill me. I'd better make sure it counts.'

The chamber became as silent as a grave as each of them realised what she was planning. Then they were all speaking at once. 'No, you can't do it, Dorian. We need you. You're our leader.'

'Not much use for a leader if there is no-one to lead.'

What a thing to say, but who could argue with her?

The faintest murmur of gunfire crept into the chamber. Was it aimed at Olanda, or was she already dead? Berrin forced himself to stare at Dorian. She shouldn't die alone, and if there were two crossbows and two deadly bolts fired at the intruders, the chances of a successful kill were doubled. 'I'll —' The words caught in his throat as he realised what he was committing himself to. He swallowed and formed his lips round the words again. 'I'll go with you.'

'Go where?' asked a voice.

They spun round sharply. Quinn had forgotten to turn off his helmet lamp. Its beam came to rest on a single body as it crawled free of the narrow pipe.

'Olanda!'

Olanda didn't wait for an answer to her question. She didn't even acknowledge the relief and sheer delight in Berrin's voice as he cried her name. She had news of her own and it wouldn't wait. 'They're moving off into another part of the system.'

'The Gadges?'

'Who else would I be talking about?' she replied sharply.

'But that creature, the probe . . .' said Berrin, helping her to her feet.

'I don't understand either,' she said and spread her hands wide. 'Maybe it's not as good at picking us up as we thought. Either that, or it's just plain stupid. Who cares. It's got those Gadges heading over that way.' She pointed to the map on the wall, a copy of the one Berrin had stolen from Gadger Red. The original stayed safe with Ferdinand, who had drawn this copy on a large square of material.

'Are you sure?'

'I tracked them myself,' Olanda snorted indignantly.

'And the probe didn't know you were close by?' Berrin prompted.

'Nope. She must have been lucky that first time. Maybe we were breathing too hard and we made it easy for her.'

Berrin would have liked to believe it, but what about Jasper? How could she have known that a tiny rat was perched on his shoulder? But such questions were forgotten as relief flooded through them all. For now, at least, they were safe again.

FIVE
Mission to the Surface

DORIAN LOOKED AROUND the expectant faces. More were arriving every minute, all with the same thrilling news. The Gadges were off on a wild-goose chase. She wasn't about to let the opportunity slip by. 'If they aren't chasing us about in the tunnels, then we can risk a mission up to the surface. It's Doomsday, remember. We have to destroy everything Malig Tumora has going up there, before he destroys us.'

There were only three people Dorian trusted to take with her on this mission.

'Wendell, you know the surface better than any of us. Olanda, you'd better bring that crossbow. And Berrin, I'll need you to keep an eye on Olanda.'

And for your courage, she might have added. The others had quickly forgotten what Berrin had said in the excitement of Olanda's news. But not Dorian. There was something about Berrin that marked him for a higher destiny. There was never any doubt that she would choose him.

THEY HAD TO WAIT UNTIL dark, but the many hours until then were not wasted. There was bread to steal from the bakery, and the muddy water that flowed through the tunnels had left them all filthy. A good wash was in order.

'I hated baths in the dormitories,' Olanda complained. 'That was one of the things I was trying to escape from.'

'You have to get the mud off or the Rhino Dogs will sniff you out,' Dorian explained, but Olanda continued her protest until Dorian said bluntly, 'Scrub yourself clean or I'll scrub you from tonight's little adventure.'

Sulking, the girl went to stand under the freezing shower created from a handy water main not far from the base.

Just after midnight, the four children climbed out through an access hole hidden beneath a clump of trees. No sign of the Gadges. Many were still underground, but so far away that they were no danger. Using the copied map, they set off for the nearest glasshouse.

This was a scouting mission only. 'Ferdinand wants to know how these glasshouses work,' Dorian had explained. 'He thinks they are too big to destroy, so we'll have to stop them from working instead.'

It had sounded easy. Now that they were on the surface, with danger at their elbow, the job looked a lot harder.

After an hour's stealthy progress, they found their destination.

'There are lights on and I can see shadows moving around inside,' Wendell reported.

He crept forward for a closer look. When he returned, he put their minds at ease. 'Grown-ups. They must have jobs inside the glasshouse. One of them was fixing a black pipe that was leaking water.'

'Will they sound the alarm?' Dorian asked Berrin.

'I don't think so. The fragrance of the flowers will be very strong inside the glasshouse. That means those grown-ups won't do anything they haven't been told to do.'

Dorian considered this good news. 'Right, listen up. Wendell and I will search around and learn what we can. Berrin, you and Olanda stand guard.'

Berrin and Olanda watched as Dorian and Wendell crossed the short distance to the glasshouse. Olanda checked her crossbow and the supply of bolts that hung from her belt. She was ready. They scampered after them and then turned to watch for any movement or strange lights approaching.

All seemed quiet. Berrin looked for the other two and spotted them crouched at the corner, discussing something they had discovered. His eyes drifted towards the glass. Inside were the flowers that had so nearly overpowered him. How could there be so many?

A dull light illuminated the building, enough for the unfortunate grown-ups to go about their duties. One passed close by as Berrin stood watching. Like the others he had seen once before, this one's eyes opened onto a deadened world.

They were still human though, with the same features as the Rats. Berrin found himself looking for similarities. That woman has a nose like Vindy's, he thought. And that man's hair matches Quinn's. Was there a connection? Was he looking at parents?

Ferdinand had told them about parents. Now, though he knew he should be keeping guard, he looked for Ferdinand's face among the grown-up workers. If he found a strong resemblance, then the man might well be his own father.

'Berrin,' came a whisper. It made him jump.

He recovered quickly and found Wendell at his side. 'We can't find much of any use here. Dorian wants to follow the pipes towards the houses. Come on.'

The pipes were as thick as Berrin's thigh and easy to follow because they were laid across the ground. A little soil had been tossed around them, to keep them in place, but there was no attempt to bury them.

'Malig Tumora didn't think there'd ever be

rebels like us,' Dorian commented and her words gave them heart.

Berrin stooped and pressed his fingers against a pipe. 'It's not made of concrete. Feel it,' he urged. 'It's flexible.'

'Ferdinand talked about this stuff,' Dorian explained. 'It's called plastic. There's all kinds and thicknesses.'

They chose one pipe and followed it, while Olanda kept careful watch along the sights of her crossbow.

'Hey, where has the pipe gone?' Dorian hissed into the darkness. It seemed to have disappeared.

'It's just run under this low bush here,' Berrin pointed out. With Wendell's help, he pulled the undergrowth aside to reveal the curved surface of the pipe. He was about to let the branches fall back into place when an idea came to him.

'Do you think we could cut it?' he asked. 'We could hide the open end under this bush and no-one would see it was broken.'

Dorian understood immediately. 'Then none of the houses downstream from the break would get their dose of gas from the flowers.'

'What would happen?' Olanda asked.

'We won't know until we try it,' said Wendell. Already, he had drawn his sword.

'Careful,' Dorian cautioned. 'Cut it slowly, like a loaf of bread.'

Wendell fell to his knees and sawed through the plastic. He had barely finished when the barking of Rhino Dogs startled them.

'Quick, there's time to get back to the tunnels,' said Wendell and jumped to his feet.

'No, wait,' whispered Dorian, calling him back. 'They're not coming this way. It sounds like they've got someone cornered.'

'A grown-up, do you think?' asked Berrin. After his recent spying through the glass, he was more intrigued by them than ever.

'We'll take a look,' Dorian decided. The other three stayed close behind her as they made their way cautiously towards the barking.

The noise was coming from among some deserted buildings. A raised walkway looked down on the scene and, with the night sky free of clouds, the moonlight let them see what was going on.

Three Rhino Dogs were gathered playfully around a figure which cowered in a doorway.

'Can you see what it is?' Olanda whispered.

She was answered by a silent shaking of heads. The shape outlined in the moonlight didn't match any creature, human or beast, they had ever seen.

As they watched, the hated shadow of a Gadge loomed up behind the raucous dogs. 'That's enough,' he called, pushing them aside roughly.

Rhino Dogs could turn mean if mistreated, as Berrin knew only too well. But these three were too afraid of the Gadge to respond. They backed away, and when he turned on them, growling like the savage wolf that he was, they ran off.

The Gadge stepped forward and pulled the unfortunate fugitive to its feet. Not that those feet looked like much use. They seemed stuck onto the end of short and spindly legs as an afterthought. No wonder the creature had been caught so easily by the Rhino Dogs.

'What are you up to?' demanded the Gadge, who clearly recognised the poor thing. 'You shouldn't be roaming about at night like this.'

'I was trying to escape,' said the odd creature defiantly, and as soon as the words left her lips, Berrin and Olanda knew who she was.

'The probe,' they whispered together.

Berrin strained to get a better look, but his eyes could barely believe what little he could see. None of the outlines made sense. What kind of animal was this? Yet she could talk. Some of her, at least, was human. He would need to get closer to discover more.

The probe turned her head and looked up towards them.

Oh no, he thought. In the faintest whisper he could manage, he spoke directly into Dorian's ear. 'She knows we're here.'

As he spoke, the probe continued to stare and this time her head nodded slightly, twice, up and down. It was not enough for the Gadge to notice, but for the four Rats hiding on the walkway, the signal was clear.

Olanda took a bolt from her waistband and fitted it to the crossbow. Hours earlier, they had decided to kill this creature, even if some of them had to die to get the job done. Now they had a far easier opportunity. Olanda took aim.

Berrin couldn't let it happen. He put his hand on Olanda's shoulder. 'Wait. She hasn't given us away to the Gadge,' he whispered.

As soon as he had said this, the probe spoke up loudly, as though responding to Berrin's words. 'I don't want to work for you Gadges any more.'

'You don't, eh?' snarled her captor. He grabbed her brutally and shoved her out in front of him. 'Well, Malig Tumora has no use for you otherwise. That's the only reason he created you, to search out his enemies, and that includes those little nuisances underground.'

'I'm not going back into those tunnels,' the probe said. 'I've listened to Malig Tumora giving orders to Gadger Red. He wants them all killed and quickly. Well, I've heard those little humans talking in the tunnels and I don't want to help you kill them.'

As the creature spoke, Olanda lined up her shot. Berrin couldn't bear to watch what was about to happen. He turned away as Wendell whispered, 'Are you ready?'

The probe looked up at the walkway again. She was as easy a target as she would ever be. Olanda's finger rested on the trigger.

'What is it? What's up there?' said the Gadge suspiciously. He turned to follow the probe's gaze.

'Now,' Dorian breathed to Olanda.

Berrin saw the gentle squeezing of Olanda's finger and the bow's shudder as the bolt was sent on its way. Moments later, he heard the thud of impact and a strangled grunt of pain. It lasted only a second before the shocking silence of death.

SIX

To Kill in Cold Blood

BERRIN HADN'T BEEN ABLE to watch, but Dorian and Wendell were not as squeamish. Now that it was done, they were already on the move.

But the Gadge, thought Berrin. It would be furious that they had killed its prisoner. Wouldn't it be looking for them right now? Surely the best thing was for Olanda to load up her crossbow again.

When he dared to look, what he saw changed everything.

Olanda noticed his surprise. 'You thought I was aiming at the probe, didn't you?'

Berrin nodded, still taking in the scene of death on the street below.

'Nah, the Gadge had to go first,' she said calmly. 'Never miss a chance to kill one of them. Come on.'

She followed the other two down the walkway and onto the street. Berrin stumbled after them.

'Good shooting,' said Dorian, who was inspecting the dead Gadge. It lay on its back, arms outstretched, the bolt protruding from its chest.

'Right through the heart,' Wendell added with genuine admiration.

Olanda was pleased and looked to Berrin for similar praise. But he had turned his attention to the terrified probe.

He could see the creature clearly now, though it was not a pretty sight. The head might have been borrowed from a small dog, though the ears were strangely uncovered by fur or even a flap of skin. Her eyes were huge and very round. They darted in fear from one Rat to another. When she opened her mouth, a thick tongue protruded, its tip tapering to a fine point that curled into a tight spiral. The skin around her face and along her arms was scaly, like a lizard's. Yet her hands were huge, with a web of skin between the fingers.

The strangest sight, though, were the wings. They were far too small to lift her into the air. Were they just for decoration? If so, they failed. The probe was the ugliest creature Berrin could ever have imagined, awake or in his dreams.

'Who . . . who are you?' she asked them.

'I'm sure you can guess,' said Dorian. 'The real question is, *what* are you?'

'I'm a probe,' she answered miserably.

'You've been down in our tunnels. These two were nearly killed because of you. In fact, the Gadges were using you to track us all down.'

'Yes, it's true. They took me underground to find you.' The creature became distracted when Wendell reached for Olanda's crossbow. 'What are you going to do with me?'

'Kill you,' Wendell answered simply. 'You're too dangerous to live.' As he spoke, he wound back the string of the crossbow. All he needed now was a bolt from Olanda's waistband.

Terror showed in the probe's face, but there was a kind of acceptance too, as though she understood why they had to do it. 'There's no need to kill me,' she said, fighting to control her fear. 'I'm going to escape. I want to get away from Malig Tumora, forever.'

'Not on those legs, you're not,' said Dorian, inspecting her more closely.

It was true. The probe could only move with an awkward waddle, like a duck, and she was rather fat around the middle. Those little legs were too frail to carry her far, and as for running to avoid Rhino Dogs and the more frightening beasts that occasionally roamed these streets . . .

'Where will you go?' Dorian asked, a surprising note of concern in her voice.

'I don't know. I just want to get away from here so Malig Tumora can't reach me.'

'Don't we all,' said Olanda, earning a laugh from Wendell.

The smile died on his face as he hefted the crossbow in his hands. 'We can't let her go, Dorian, if that's what you're thinking. She'll be back in Malig Tumora's hands by morning. Don't forget the strange gifts she has.'

Berrin's own confusion was unbearable. Should they kill her? Could they afford to let her go free? Then he remembered how they had doubted the probe's abilities. 'How good are you — at listening and smelling, I mean? How well can you track us down in the tunnels?'

The creature didn't want to answer at first. Hardly surprising, with Wendell ready to put a bolt through her heart just as Olanda had done to the Gadge. But mixed in with her reluctance was a need to explain.

'I could hear you talking, even your whispers,' she said honestly. 'Malig Tumora made me, and others like me, to spy on the people up here on the surface, the ones you call grown-ups. He's always afraid some of them will rise up against him. He doesn't realise it, but I can hear him speaking too. That's how I know what animals he mixed together to make us the way we are. Vultures, so that we can see eight times better than humans. A special breed of dog so that we smell things forty times better. My tongue lets me taste the air like a butterfly. I can hear like a bat, sense sunlight like a bee and feel heat like a snake. I hate him,' she went on, her voice suddenly fierce with anger.

'Once, there were seven of us, you know, but I am the only one left.'

'The last of your kind,' muttered Berrin who was beginning to pity the probe more than he feared her powerful senses.

'Just as well,' Wendell said unkindly.

The probe looked at him defiantly. 'I don't really care whether you kill me. One way or another, I won't help Malig Tumora ever again.'

'We can't kill her,' Berrin said. 'Not in cold blood.'

'Don't be a fool,' Wendell snapped. 'It's easy for her to say these things now, hoping we will spare her. As soon as she is back in Malig Tumora's clutches, she will change sides again.'

'Then let's take her down into the tunnels with us.'

Even Olanda gasped at this suggestion. 'But it's not even a day since she was down there helping the Gadges.'

'I'd rather help you,' the probe said.

'It's a trick,' said Wendell. 'Gadger Red has put her up to this. He wants us to take her down into the pipes so she can find our base.'

The probe shook her head. Tears of frustration and grief spilled from her large, liquid eyes.

'Well, what are we going to do?' Wendell demanded. 'There will be more Gadges along in a minute. We can't stand here all night.'

'Take her with us,' said Berrin firmly.

Olanda didn't look quite so convinced, but she stood by her friend. In the end, though, it was up to Dorian.

She took the crossbow from Wendell's hands, careful not to get her fingers in the way of the cocked string in case it fired. 'Today, you were tracking us through the tunnels,' she began. 'But you didn't lead the Gadges to our base.'

The probe shook her head slowly.

'You knew where it was, though, didn't you?'

Dorian's three companions gasped, even Wendell, who thought he had guessed everything they needed to know about this sad creature.

The response was a long time coming, but finally the creature nodded her fox-like head.

'Then you led them away on purpose. Is that right?'

Again, she nodded.

'Why?'

'Because I heard you young humans speaking. I realised how much you all look out for one another, how you want to rescue your kind from Malig Tumora.'

'That's it, then,' said Dorian, handing the crossbow to Olanda. 'We'll take her with us. Who knows, she might end up the best Rat we've ever had.'

SEVEN
Blackout

'THE BEST RAT WE'VE ever had?' snarled Wendell. 'She'll get us all killed.'

He had a point, Berrin realised. The probe could only move slowly and that was the last quality a Rat should have if she and her companions wanted to stay alive. The journey back to the tunnels was a frustrating one. They were lucky that no Gadges appeared.

'Where are they?' Dorian asked the probe.

The creature listened for a few moments. She even kneeled on the ground and spread her grotesque hands in the dirt. 'I can't pick them up,' she said with a shake of the head.

'My senses don't work quite as well out in the open. Down in your tunnels is where they work best.'

'We know,' said Wendell, ungraciously.

They were particularly careful once they had re-entered the tunnels.

'You don't need to worry,' the probe told them. 'There are no Gadges nearby. I can't hear any at all, in fact.'

'Where have they gone?' Berrin asked. It didn't make sense. The Gadges had light to see by now and guns as well. Even without the probe to guide them, they had the advantage. 'Why aren't they down here, working their way through the tunnels, looking for us?'

'I was thinking the same thing,' said Dorian suspiciously. The beam of her helmet lamp fell onto the probe, who stared back at her timidly. But Dorian had made her decision about this odd creature. She was no spy. 'Come on. It's a long way to base yet.'

It was indeed a long journey through the tunnels, made tediously slow by the probe's short legs. The other Rats were stirring for the new day by the time they arrived.

'We'd better take you into the sleeping chamber and find you a bed,' said Dorian.

But when the probe tried to follow Dorian into the narrow tunnel, she became wedged in the opening.

The waking Rats had heard the voices and came out to investigate. 'What's *that*?' a voice asked out of the darkness.

'Don't be cruel,' Dorian scolded the speaker. She quickly explained who they had brought with them and why.

Quinn never stayed quiet for long. 'What's your name then?' he inquired.

'Name?' said the probe.

'Yeah. I'm Quinn and that's Berrin standing beside you.' He pointed towards another figure. 'And underneath all that dirt is a girl called Olanda.'

Olanda was quick to rise to the bait. '*You* can talk, Quinn. Whenever you crawl through a narrow pipe, you end up adding more mud than you scrape off.'

The probe paid no attention to this friendly teasing. 'Name?' she repeated. 'I'm a probe. I don't have one. I mean ... no-one ever gave me one.'

They stared at her, astonished. No name. How could any creature, even one that looked as odd as this, live without a name?

'What are we going to do with her?' asked Berrin.

What *were* they going to do with her? 'Ferdinand will have to decide,' said Dorian. 'We'll take her down to see him.'

'No,' said Wendell sharply. 'We're not sure of her yet. She shouldn't know where ...' He left the rest unsaid, reluctant to repeat the revered name.

Berrin kept his gaze on the nameless probe. She didn't speak, but he could read what she was thinking in her eyes. She already knew where Ferdinand lived. She could probably hear his breathing, or even the beat of his heart, but she had enough sense not to say so.

Dorian and Wendell stood scowling at each other. Then Berrin realised it was all about nothing anyway. 'The probe can't meet ... him,' he said, avoiding the name a second time. 'She can't fit through the pipes.'

That settled it. Dorian took Berrin with her down to Ferdinand instead. He was pleased to see them both. Berrin had brought Jasper too and Ferdinand was delighted to have the rat perched on his shoulder again.

Dorian gave her report of their mission, speaking eagerly of how they had cut the pipe that carried the flowers' fragrance to a row of houses.

'Fantastic,' said Ferdinand. 'And the break is hidden under a tree. Even better. In a day or two, I want you to send a patrol up to the same area. If I am right, some of the grown-ups will be shaking off the effects of the flowers by then. We have to know what happens.'

The excitement of this news quickly left his face. 'We need a bit of good luck, don't we? The last day or two have been tough. I was worried we would lose some of the children. Or that the Gadges would find the base.'

'They haven't even come close yet,' Dorian told him confidently.

Ferdinand was clearly relieved. 'Quinn told me some wild story about a special weapon the Gadges had with them. Something that could see through the pipes and pinpoint where we were hiding.'

Dorian shared a worried glance with Berrin, then told Ferdinand the rest of the story about the night's mission to the surface.

'You brought her down here?' Ferdinand asked, his eyes wide. But he relaxed again just as quickly. 'I'm sure you know what you're doing, Dorian. What about you, Berrin, do you think she will betray us?'

'No,' Berrin said immediately. 'I listened to her voice when she told us how much she hates Malig Tumora. A gentle creature like her couldn't fake feelings as strong at that.'

'A good answer,' Ferdinand said with a smile. 'It doesn't surprise me that she hates Malig Tumora. From the way you describe her, she sounds rather ugly. Poor thing. I'll bet she knows it too. Of course she hates the one who made her like that.'

'How could he do it?' Berrin asked.

'How *could* he do it or how *did* he do it?' said Ferdinand, deliberately playing with Berrin's words. 'They are two separate questions. I know you, Berrin,' he said, leaning forward to place a comforting hand on the boy's shoulder. 'You care about her, don't you?

You know how cruel it is to let her live her life like a monster.'

Ferdinand paused. He was sitting on the cushions that were his only comfort in his stuffy prison. 'I told you that Malig Tumora was a great scientist. But there have been many others before him, some so clever that they could make anything they wanted to.'

'They didn't, though,' said Berrin, jumping in eagerly because he had guessed what was to come.

'No, they didn't,' Ferdinand agreed. 'Despite all their powers, they always asked themselves some important questions first. Should I do this? Is it right? Is it good? But Malig Tumora — I doubt he has ever stopped to ask those questions.'

'How does he do it? How does he make strange animals like that probe?' Dorian asked.

'He uses genes,' Ferdinand answered. 'Every kind of animal, even human beings, have these genes. Genes make us what we are, how we look. They even decide what we can do. Malig Tumora has found a way to mix them up to create whatever he wants.'

'The Gadges,' said Dorian.

'Yes, half wolf and half man.'

In his mind, Berrin raced through the many beasts he had encountered. Such strange combinations, and the poor probe was the most outrageous of all. 'She's the last of her kind,' he told Ferdinand.

'It doesn't surprise me,' Ferdinand replied with a sigh. 'Few of Malig Tumora's experiments survive, even in his laboratory. Our new recruit sounds brave, but I doubt she will be able to live for very long in these tunnels.'

A terrible thought entered Berrin's mind. The probe could probably hear every word they were saying and Ferdinand had just predicted her death. Sadness speared through him. In the heat of their battle against Malig Tumora and the Gadges, it was easy to forget such feelings.

He drew his sword from behind his back and, while the other two watched in confusion, began to scrape it loudly across the concrete. With the sound masking his voice, he leaned forward and whispered into Ferdinand's ear.

After a few moments, Ferdinand was smiling. 'Yes, I understand.' He thought hard, closing his eyes for extra concentration. His face softened, as though he was remembering a happier time in his life. Then he took the sword from Berrin and kept up the masking sound while he whispered a reply into the boy's ear. 'Take good care of her,' he said finally.

It was time to return to the base. Ferdinand stood up, though he could never stand up completely. How he must want to stretch out and hold his hands above his head, Berrin thought.

They made their way to the end of Ferdinand's tiny home. Dorian and Berrin hadn't turned on their helmet lamps yet. Light came from the bulb overhead. As Ferdinand opened his mouth to say goodbye, the light bulb went out.

'Blackout,' said Dorian.

Berrin had never heard the word before, but he knew instantly what it meant. The light bulb that brought life and a little warmth to Ferdinand's prison had suddenly died and the world had indeed gone black.

'No, my guess is that this is more than a simple blackout,' Ferdinand told them. 'The Gadges have found where we tap into the electrical power lines.'

Silence followed as they dared to imagine what this meant.

Dorian snapped on her helmet light, but when Berrin did the same, she rounded on him. 'Turn it off,' she insisted. 'We'll need to conserve every moment of battery power we have left. Until we can get the electricity flowing again, we can't recharge anything. Come on, we'd better get back to the base. Follow me and stay close.'

They crawled away, too worried for even a word of farewell for Ferdinand.

EIGHT
A New and Deadly Foe

BACK AT THE BASE, Dorian and Berrin found that Wendell had already ordered the helmet lamps turned off.

'It's a bit suspicious, don't you think?' he goaded Dorian. 'That this should happen now, I mean, right after we've brought Malig Tumora's probe into our headquarters.'

'I'm not Malig Tumora's any more,' the probe's gentle voice insisted out of the darkness. 'I was escaping when you found me. It was no trick.'

'You're a spy!' Wendell shouted. 'You're sending some kind of signal to the Gadges right now, aren't you?'

'Stop it, Wendell!' Dorian cried. 'The probe is one of us now.'

There was no reply, and in the blackness it was impossible to read Wendell's face.

'There are no Gadges in these tunnels, I promise you,' said the probe. 'But there is something else.'

This would have been alarming news even if the lights were on. In the darkness, it sounded especially ominous.

'What is it?' Berrin asked for them all.

'I'm not sure. I've been listening to it for a few minutes now. It's still a long way off.'

'Well, that's a relief,' said Quinn. 'How do you know it's not just a Gadge?'

The probe didn't answer straightaway. Though they couldn't see her, they could hear as she moved to the side of the tunnel and placed her huge hands firmly against the concrete.

'It's not walking on two legs,' she told them tentatively. 'It's not walking on four, either. I've never heard anything like it before, except . . .'

The pause that followed only made them more anxious. 'Except what?' Dorian demanded.

'I hear all sorts of things that you don't, like the sound of spiders walking.'

Another pause, this time loaded with dread.

'Eight legs. You mean this new thing in the tunnels is a spider?' Dorian asked.

'I hate spiders,' said Olanda, as though she was choosing a pet.

'It's not a spider,' the probe decided. 'Just something like it.'

'How big?' asked Dorian. She needed all the facts so she could decide on the best thing to do.

'I can't tell yet. Wait!' the probe cried suddenly. 'It's moving, moving very fast, faster than any Gadge could run.'

'It's a Dodgem,' said Ruben. 'All the bumps and rattles they make have confused you. One of us is out there on patrol in a Dodgem.'

For a moment, they all believed him. Maybe they *wanted* to believe him. Besides, they all knew that Dodgems were the only things that could travel quickly along the tunnels.

'All our Dodgems are here at the base,' said Quinn.

'It's turned off the main tunnels,' the probe continued. 'Now it's turning again, into a smaller one still. I can tell by the change in the echo.'

'Small tunnels. You mean the ones we crawl along on our hands and knees?' asked Berrin.

'Yes, and it's going just as fast in those as it did in the biggest tunnels.'

Berrin wondered if his was the only mouth that had suddenly gone as dry as dust.

'We have to know what it is,' Dorian announced. 'Wendell, Berrin — take one of the Dodgems.'

'They'll run down its battery,' someone pointed out.

'That doesn't matter. Whatever the creature is, it's fast and it's small enough to go anywhere we can go. Even down to Ferdinand's sanctuary. We have to know how serious the danger is.'

WENDELL TOOK THE DRIVER'S seat. Berrin was glad. If they had been going to intercept a Gadge, he would have known what to expect. If they were heading up to the surface, he could have prepared himself. But not this time. He only hoped he had the courage for a mission into the unknown.

Thankfully, Wendell seemed undaunted. 'That

probe friend of yours said the spider was this way, about three kilometres.'

'It's not a spider. Just something like it,' Berrin repeated under his breath.

They shot quickly through a large tunnel then more cautiously along a smaller one. It was here, with little room to spare, that the Dodgem stopped.

'What's wrong?' Berrin asked.

'Don't know. The stupid thing just stopped.'

They climbed out to inspect it. The headlight had died as well, but they still had their helmet lamps. Berrin had learned enough about these fabulous Dodgem machines to know that the batteries were linked to the motor by two thick wires, one red, the other blue. The blue one had broken away from a coupling on the battery. With his helmet beam focused on the spot, he reached down to fix it.

Before he could touch it, Wendell put his hand on his arm. 'What's that noise?'

Berrin strained his ears. He could hear it too. It was growing louder even as they sat there listening. 'Whatever it is, it's in this tunnel and heading our way.'

'The thing we've come looking for?'

'What else could it be?' Berrin asked.

They stared into the gloom. The weak light of their helmet lamps barely made an impression. There was no light coming from whatever approached them, but it was moving quickly. Wendell unhooked the crossbow from its rack. He just had time to haul back the string and slip a bolt into place before Berrin gasped.

They were the first Rats to set eyes on their new enemy. The probe had been right. It wasn't a spider. Just something like one.

Berrin found himself staring at a giant scorpion.

THE SCORPION CAME TO a halt twenty metres from the Dodgem. In those few moments, Berrin took in every detail. The shiny blue body was low to the ground and protected by a series of armoured plates, each overlapping the next. There were legs, four on each side, as the probe had predicted. But there was something else as well. Wheels. Berrin knew instantly that this was no animal, like the Gadges or the Rhino Dogs. This was a machine.

If he had doubted it, the 'eyes' on the front would have settled the matter for him. They glowed red. That was how it knew they were there, he realised. It was picking up their body heat. In Berrin's mind, though, it was still a scorpion. It had one feature that would always link it to the real ones he had seen scuttling about in the pipes: its tail.

As the scorpion advanced towards them, using its legs now instead of the wheels, that tail reared up menacingly. But it didn't have the sharp point of a stinger at the end. No, at the tip of this scorpion's tail, he could make out a hole, two centimetres across.

'Wendell, watch out!' he screamed. 'Its tail is some kind of cannon.'

Wendell was already taking aim. As Berrin called out, he sent a bolt hurtling towards the scorpion. It bounced off its armour harmlessly. Then the scorpion fired back.

The sound was deafening; the impact devastating. The single shot from the scorpion's tail destroyed the front of the Dodgem and threw it back against the two boys sheltering behind it. Berrin just managed to pull Wendell free before the motor and battery burst into flames.

Wendell wasn't badly hurt, but he barely knew where he was.

'This way. We have to get as far down the pipe as possible,' Berrin called, dragging Wendell's limp body away from the flames. The pipe was narrow and made movement awkward. He looked up and found they had only retreated ten metres. The scorpion would advance on them at any moment. One direct hit from that deadly tail and they were history.

Back along the tunnel, he could see the scorpion on the move. It had already reached the burning wreck of the Dodgem. The flames offered no threat to its protective shell. But as Berrin watched, waiting for the *boom* of its cannon, expecting the sound to be the last he ever heard, he found a moment of hope. The twisted metal was an obstacle the scorpion could not get round.

If we can only get out of its line of fire, he thought.

Another ten metres of desperate hauling and he had Wendell at a junction. He was slowly regaining his senses. 'What ... what happened?'

'No time for that now,' Berrin told him. 'This way, quickly!'

A second explosion rocked the tunnels. The shot hadn't been aimed at them, though, or they would be dead. A third ear-splitting crash shuddered through every inch of Berrin's body. The Dodgem. It was firing at the Dodgem, blowing it to pieces, so it could come after them.

Wendell was almost himself now, but he was bleeding from the head and he couldn't put any weight on his right arm. Somehow, they struggled on, Berrin providing the energy for both of them. They reached another T-junction and by then Wendell had had enough. 'I have to rest,' he pleaded.

But Berrin took no notice. Which way? Left or right? He chose the left. That simple decision, taken quickly and without a moment's thought, would save their lives.

NINE
A Gift for a Saviour

WENDELL FOUND THE STRENGTH to drag himself ten metres along the pipe, then twenty, but that was it. He flopped, exhausted, onto the muddy concrete and no amount of prodding or pulling from Berrin would move him.

Berrin was still trying when another explosion thundered through the pipes. When the echo had died, a new sound took its place, one he had heard only briefly before. The scorpion was on the move again.

Berrin flicked off his helmet lamp, then Wendell's too. In total darkness, he listened as the whirring of its motor grew louder. It had followed their trail at the first corner. Had it seen them go that way or was it using its heat sensors?

In a matter of seconds, the scorpion was at the T-junction only twenty metres away. They had no crossbow. Wendell had dropped it back at the Dodgem. As for swords, what use were they against an armoured shell? The scorpion would finish them with a single shot from its tail.

A clicking sound joined the whirring. Muddy gravel popped and grated as the scorpion turned, first to the right, then to the left. It would be using its heat sensors now.

Then it was on the move again. Berrin's heart felt as if it was trying to jump out through his throat. They wouldn't see the scorpion coming. The flash of its cannon would be the last light they saw.

But the noise was growing fainter. The scorpion had turned to the right at the T-junction. It wasn't coming towards them. It was heading away.

They were safe for now, but Berrin guessed this was only a brief reprieve. The scorpion hadn't gone far. It was beginning a search of each pipe it came to, like the machine it was. It was only a matter of time before it tracked back to the T-junction to search in the opposite direction.

'Wendell, can you move?' Berrin whispered.

'I'll try.' Wendell struggled painfully on, but twenty metres was as far as he could go before his muscles demanded more rest. 'You go on ahead, Berrin. Get back to base if you can and tell them about this thing. Tell them it's a robot,' he said, using a word Berrin had never heard before.

Wendell had saved Berrin's life when the Dfx tied him to a stake for the Crocodilian to eat. He couldn't abandon him now. They would die together. And their death wasn't far off, it seemed.

'What's that?' Wendell asked, not for the first time that day.

Berrin could hear that it was a machine. It wasn't coming from the T-junction, but that didn't mean much. The sound grew louder. They had no plan, no weapons, no hope.

Along the distant tunnel, Berrin thought he detected a dim light. No, it couldn't be. The scorpion didn't need light to find its way around. The light became stronger. There was no doubt now; it wasn't his imagination.

He dared to hope, just for a moment. Then it appeared, a Dodgem, its powerful headlight flooding the narrow pipe so that Berrin had to put his hand up to protect his eyes.

'Berrin?' a voice called as the Dodgem came to a halt just in front of them. It was Quinn.

Now there was a second light racing towards them. Another Dodgem, this one with Olanda at the wheel.

'Quickly, help me get Wendell into a Dodgem,' Berrin called.

The three Rats heaved and groaned in the narrow space. Wendell didn't measure down any more and it was no easy feat getting someone his size into a Dodgem, even when he wasn't injured. Then Berrin heard a sound that made his blood run cold.

He turned to stare up the tunnel. The Dodgem's headlight was still on, illuminating the tunnel all the way to the junction. There it was, the scorpion. It had dropped onto its eight legs and was steadying itself ready to shoot. As Berrin watched, its tail arched up over its back, until the short barrel of its cannon pointed at them.

Quinn had seen it too. Without a word, he took the crossbow from his Dodgem.

'It's no use,' Berrin warned him. 'The armour is too thick. And watch out for that tail. It's some sort of gun.'

Despite his fear, Berrin continued to shove Wendell into the Dodgem's seat. There, it was done, not that it mattered. The scorpion would surely fire any moment now. He turned around just as Quinn released the bolt from his crossbow. Berrin knew it was useless against the scorpion's hard shell. Worse, Quinn had aimed rather badly. The bolt flew well above the robot's twin red eyes.

Then he heard a dull *thunk*. The arrow had hit something after all. With his helmet light back on, Berrin looked for the impact. Were his eyes playing tricks? No, he stared even harder and knew it was true. The bolt had lodged in the barrel of the cannon, like a cork in a bottle.

The scorpion didn't fire. Instead, more clicks and whirring filled the tunnel. Berrin was amazed to see one of the red eyes rise upwards on the end of a stalk. The tail pressed forward and the eye swivelled on the end of its stalk to inspect the damage.

'Quick, into the Dodgems while it decides what to do,' Olanda called.

Berrin scrambled and squeezed past the nearest Dodgem, groping his way to the second until he fell into the seat behind Olanda. He looked back to see Quinn doing the same. They were ready to go and still the scorpion hadn't fired. Berrin looked beyond Quinn to where it had stood, but the tunnel was empty.

'HOW DID YOU KNOW WE were in trouble?' Berrin shouted to Olanda, who seemed determined to challenge Quinn for the title of Most Reckless Dodgem Driver.

'The probe,' she yelled back. 'She told us where you were. Insisted we take two Dodgems. She said yours was badly damaged.'

'Damaged! It was blown apart.'

'What *was* that thing?' Olanda cried.

'I don't know, but I can guess who made it.'

AT THE BASE, QUINN WAS a hero. Berrin described how his shot from the crossbow had disabled the scorpion. 'A miracle,' he called it, and who would argue with him?

'Did you really aim at that tiny opening?' Olanda asked. She was no mean shot with a crossbow herself these days and marvelled at such skill.

Quinn grinned from ear to ear as they praised him. 'Yes, I aimed for the cannon,' he assured them.

'But what are the chances you could ever do it again?' Dorian asked.

Quinn's smile widened even further. 'One in a hundred, maybe. I just hope I don't have to try a second time.'

They all swallowed a little harder when they heard this. 'That scorpion will be back, that's for sure,' said Berrin. 'We'd better be ready for it.'

Before they faced this problem, they had to help Wendell out of the Dodgem. He groaned as they took his arm, but it didn't seem broken. Dorian held a cloth to the cut above his ear.

'I'm all right,' said Wendell. He cautiously let go of the pair who were holding him upright. 'I thought we were going to die in that tunnel. Just as well Dorian sent those two out to scout around.'

'I didn't,' she said. 'Not until the probe told me what had happened to you.'

'The probe,' he repeated suspiciously.

Dorian nodded, but didn't say what she might have said. She didn't need to. The others were all thinking the same thing. Wendell knew it too.

'You saved us then,' he said to the probe.

'I helped a little, maybe,' she answered modestly.

'More than a little,' he said. The suspicion and anger had left his voice at last. 'I've been hard on you. Maybe I was wrong. No,' he said immediately, straightening up as best he could. 'Not maybe. I *was* wrong. Berrin and I owe you our lives. If Quinn hadn't arrived when he did, miracle shot or not, we were dead ducks. I wish ... I wish there was something I could give you.'

But there was nothing. These tunnels were no place to find gifts. No, there was nothing they could put in her hand, Berrin thought, but he was remembering his whispered conversation with Ferdinand. Now was the time to speak.

'I have something for the probe,' he said.

They all turned in surprise, eager to see what he had found to give her.

'It's nothing you can see or touch,' he announced, teasing them a little and enjoying every second of it. 'I asked Ferdinand to help me choose it, and he came up with the perfect thing.'

He turned to the probe. 'It's a name,' he said. 'We're going to call you Belle. It means beautiful.'

TEN

The Scorpion Returns

'BELLE.' THE PROBE SAID it again and again, as though the word had become a precious stone and she was turning it over in her fingers. To hear it was to see it. For a creature with such finely tuned senses, perhaps that was true.

'My own name. Thank you,' she said to Berrin. 'Thank you so much. This is the first thing anyone has ever given me. I love it.'

'It was Ferdinand who came up with the name.'

'Yes, but it was your idea, wasn't it?'

Berrin blushed a little and there was just enough light from Dorian's lamp for the others to see. Olanda couldn't resist the chance to tease. 'It means beautiful,' she repeated, rolling her eyes.

'Ferdinand also told me that Olanda means girl with dirty face,' Berrin shot back at her. Not that he had managed to insult Olanda. She replied just as quickly, 'It suits me then.'

There was no time to celebrate Belle's naming. 'The Gadges will take my bolt out of the scorpion's cannon and then it will be back,' Quinn predicted.

They knew he was right. Less than an hour had passed before Belle's specially shaped ears twitched.

'It's the scorpion, isn't it?' Dorian asked. 'Which way is it heading?'

Belle listened with her hand on the wall of the pipe. Waiting for her response was agony. 'Not this way,' she said finally. 'At least, not at the moment. It's travelling quickly, following each new tunnel that it comes to and then tracking backwards to where it started. It's searching for something.'

'Yes, for us, and if it keeps going like that, eventually it will find us.'

'It will find Ferdinand too,' added Wendell, who was no longer reluctant to say the name in front of Belle.

'We'd better go down and see him,' Dorian decided. 'With the electricity cut off, all he has is a helmet lamp and the battery will be low by now.'

Berrin was again invited to join them. Quinn and Olanda crawled along the tunnel behind him, while Dorian led the way. It was a tight fit for her in the smallest pipe. The hips of her pants were starting to fray where they grazed constantly against the concrete.

Ferdinand was pleased to see them.

'Here's a new battery for your helmet lamp,' said Dorian. Together they fitted it in place, giving the gloomy tunnel a little more light.

'I've sent Ruben and Vindy to see what they can do about the electricity,' she told him. 'But the Gadges are keeping a careful watch. It could take days, and even then they might find the new place where we cut into the power lines.'

'Don't give up. We need electricity to survive,' Ferdinand said solemnly.

'We need it more than ever now,' Dorian went on. It was time to tell Ferdinand about the scorpion.

He listened without showing any fear, even when Quinn explained that the deadly machine was small enough to reach into this very chamber. He was particularly interested in Berrin's story about his narrow escape with Wendell. 'It didn't detect you at that junction?' he asked thoughtfully.

'No. It clicked and whirred and turned in both directions, but then it went off the other way.'

'Its heat-seeking sensors are weak then. The clicking noises you heard were probably sonar. That must be how it finds its way around.'

Sonar. Another new word.

'Bats use it,' Ferdinand explained. 'They send out a high-pitched screech that you and I can barely hear and then listen for the echo.'

'Like Belle?'

Ferdinand's face softened into a smile. 'So the probe has a name, does she? Yes, your new friend Belle uses sonar, but she seems to be far better at it than this scorpion.'

'I wish she had a cannon for a tail, like the scorpion,' Quinn muttered.

Ferdinand didn't concern himself with wishes. He was thinking deeply about what he had been told. 'A map,' he said at last. 'The scorpion is building a map into its thinking circuits.'

'Why would it be making a map? It's out to destroy us, isn't it?'

'Oh yes, but a map is a very powerful weapon. That's why we needed one of the surface if we were going to defeat Malig Tumora. How can you destroy your enemy if you don't know where to go? The Gadges had no way of knowing where they were underground, so they covered the same tunnels over and over as you led them on a merry chase. They would never have found our base. But this scorpion ... it will soon know our tunnels better than we do.'

At these words, each of them remembered the meeting they had held in this very pipe only a few days before. They had embarked on a struggle to the death with Malig Tumora. Doomsday. There would be only one winner.

But the Gadges had cut their power, they couldn't recharge their batteries and a robot scorpion was loose in the tunnels. Right now, the Rats were losing.

'We have to stop the scorpion creating this map,' Dorian decided.

Quinn carried more hope in his heart than most, but even he doubted they could manage it. 'The only way to do that is to stop it altogether,' he pointed out.

'We need an obstacle,' said Dorian.

'It blew our Dodgem to pieces with three shots from its tail.'

'Something stronger then. Thicker.'

'An access hole cover,' said Olanda.

'It's worth a try.'

DORIAN SENT THEM OUT in teams to steal the access hole covers. This wasn't easy. There were plenty of access holes, but there were plenty of Gadges too, waiting on the surface for frightened Rats to come scampering out of their tunnels as the scorpion went about its work.

The access hole covers were heavy too. (They wouldn't be much use against the scorpion's cannon if they weren't.) And when Berrin and Olanda finally found one unguarded, they discovered another problem. The covers were too big to fit through the hole they sat in. Round ones, anyway.

After another hour of looking, they found a square one and, by angling it cleverly between opposite corners, managed to drop it down into the large pipe below. What a noise!

The extra weight wore down the batteries of the Dodgem. How much longer would this one hold out? When they reached base, they found only one other team had matched their success.

'Where is the scorpion now?' Dorian asked Belle.

Belle stood up in her awkward way and waddled to the side of the tunnel. She flattened her hands against the pipe. 'Much closer,' she warned. After listening for a while, she was able to describe the cluster of pipes the scorpion was exploring.

'I know where that is,' said Quinn.

He chose a partner for the mission and, with one of the precious access hole covers on board his Dodgem, they set off.

Belle followed them with her senses.

'They've stopped,' she told the others after ten anxious minutes. 'I can hear them putting the heavy steel in place over a smaller pipe.' A little later she gave them the news that allowed a dozen pairs of lungs to release their air. 'They're on their way back.'

But no sooner had Quinn and his companion returned than a muffled explosion rumbled through the tunnels. Seconds later, another and then another. To Belle, they were thunderclaps in her ears. The Rats could see the pain creasing her face.

'Well, what happened?' Dorian asked for them all.

'The scorpion is moving again. It's in the tunnel they blocked off. It must have blown away the access hole cover.' As if this wasn't enough for the dispirited Rats to hear, Belle added immediately, 'It's coming closer.'

'Take the other cover and put it over the entrance to Ferdinand's tunnel,' Dorian told two Rats beside her.

'But it won't stop the scorpion any better than the first one,' Berrin complained.

'No, but it might buy us time. Even a few seconds could be precious,' she responded.

'Quickly. It's not far from us now,' Belle

informed them. 'It's searching this section. It will be here any minute.'

'We have to move or it will kill us where we stand,' said Dorian. 'Belle, guide us away from where it's searching.'

'But our stuff! The hammocks and our spare weapons,' said Quinn.

'There's no time to move them. The only things we can move are the Dodgems and ourselves.'

On Dorian's order, the Rats abandoned the base, following Belle's directions as she tracked the scorpion's relentless approach.

'Take us to tunnels the scorpion has already searched,' said Dorian.

The sorry collection of Rats followed behind, some, like Berrin and Olanda, in the last of the Dodgems that could still move. They were on the run from an enemy they had no weapons to fight and no way to stop for more than a few seconds at a time. It seemed an ominous hint of the defeat that was rapidly descending on them. Doomsday.

Belle did her job. They were safe from the scorpion for now, but as they huddled in the darkness, every light off to conserve power, they heard the destruction begin. The scorpion had finally found their base and blast followed blast as everything the Rats had collected over the years to make their lives more comfortable was destroyed. There was nothing they could do but listen.

Then the explosions stopped.

'Where is the scorpion now, Belle?' Dorian asked.

Belle took her time answering. In the end, it was Berrin who realised why. She knew where it was heading, but she didn't want to say. The scorpion was making its way towards Ferdinand's lonely prison.

Berrin slipped into the driver's seat of a Dodgem. Olanda had sensed his movement and she jumped in behind him, just as he pushed down on the lever and sent the Dodgem shooting forward. They had no idea what they were going to do, but that didn't seem to matter. If nothing else, Ferdinand would not die alone.

ELEVEN
Sector Nine

THE SCORPION DIDN'T KNOW where Ferdinand was. It didn't need to. The robot had been sent on a search-and-destroy mission to every corner of the tunnel system. Now it was only a few tunnels away from the Rats' founder.

'The access hole cover they put in its way won't last ten seconds,' Olanda called from the rear of the Dodgem.

'I know. We'll have to make sure it never reaches that far.' Berrin just wished he knew how they were going to do it. The only solution was to offer themselves as decoys.

He slowed the Dodgem as they approached a major junction. To the right lay the base, or, at least, what was left of it. In the opposite direction lay Ferdinand's vulnerable home.

They turned left and crept along, no faster than they could crawl. Their senses could hardly compare with Belle's. They could have done with her now, when the scorpion might be only metres away, around a bend in the pipe.

Then a stroke of luck. As they approached a T-junction along the stem of the T, they caught a brief glimpse of the scorpion as it shot past.

'Did it see us?' Olanda whispered.

Berrin remembered what Ferdinand had said. 'It uses heat-seeking sensors and sonar instead of eyes.'

'Thanks for the lesson,' said Olanda sharply. 'Did it detect us as it went past? That's all that matters.'

They jumped out of the Dodgem and rigged it to run in the opposite direction. 'Its sensors were too weak to find Wendell and me from twenty metres,' said Berrin as he removed the Dodgem's headlight and slotted it into place at the other end. 'This light is a different matter, though. Quick, get in,' he urged, taking the driver's seat again.

Just as he grabbed hold of the lever, the scorpion turned into the tunnel behind them. It was a chase now. They had been chased by Gadges only days before, but Gadges were animals and they grew tired and out of breath. The scorpion was a machine. But there was something about the robot that worried Berrin far more. Unlike the Gadges, a scorpion could fire on the run.

A single shot would cause enough damage to make the Dodgem stop. It might even kill them. Same thing, really. Once they stopped, the scorpion would have them at its mercy and both of them knew there would be no mercy from a machine.

As though it had read their thoughts, the scorpion fired.

The missile sailed by Berrin's ear. He didn't see it, of course, but his tangled hair suddenly flicked to the other side of his head. Moments later, the tunnel in front of them exploded. He knew instantly that they couldn't continue much further along this pipe.

There would be broken concrete on the floor and the dust would leave him blinded. As well, the scorpion was surely lining up a second shot. He had only seconds to decide, only seconds to hope for some means of escape.

'There!' shouted Olanda. 'That opening to the right.'

Berrin threw the Dodgem into a desperate turn, just as another shot from the scorpion whizzed by. Once they had straightened up, he flattened the lever as far forward as it would go. No Dodgem had ever travelled this fast. Too fast to stop if there was an obstacle ahead. Even a sharp bend would see them roll over.

The scorpion followed them, but it wasn't getting any closer. The buffeting of its wheels on the concrete made it shake as much as the Dodgem it was chasing. Though its tail was arched over its back, the vibration was too great to risk a shot.

'Berrin, do you know where this pipe leads?' Olanda shouted.

'I haven't got a clue.'

'I have,' she yelled back. 'Sector Nine.'

For an instant, Berrin's steering faltered and he almost smeared them across the tunnel wall.

'Hey, watch it! You're supposed to be the safe driver, remember,' Olanda scolded, as they settled again onto a steady course along the bottom of the pipe.

'Are you sure it's Sector Nine?' He didn't bother waiting for an answer. 'We're heading straight for the Firedrake then.'

As these words were whipped from his mouth, he found the Dodgem careering into a smooth curve. At this speed, he was forced to steer the Dodgem up onto the tunnel wall. It also meant he couldn't see far enough ahead to anticipate danger.

As they came out of the curve, the pipe branched in a Y-junction immediately in front of them. If he had tried to steer into one opening or the other, he would probably have struck the centre and killed them both. But before he knew it, the Dodgem had shot into the left-hand tunnel.

A long straight stretch followed. Olanda looked around, using her helmet lamp to stare behind them. 'Berrin,' she called excitedly. 'It went the other way.'

He had to slow the Dodgem here anyway, because water lay ahead, as far as they could see.

No sign of the scorpion. Olanda was right. He stopped altogether, to give them a few moments to think. 'How long before it finds us?'

Olanda didn't answer. Forward, back? She was trying to make up her mind. The tunnel stretched out before them until the light from the Dodgem became dim. But beyond that, a sudden brightness caught her eye. Orange, yellow, red. It was a flame. Rumbling after it, came a low, frightening roar.

'You know that Firedrake thing,' Olanda said. 'I think it just burped.'

More than that, it was coming their way and much faster than they dared think about.

'Maybe we should leave,' said Berrin. It wasn't a question.

Olanda had already turned her seat around. Berrin did the same. The light still had to be moved to the other end, but, just like last time, the catch that held it in place wouldn't release.

'Come on,' Olanda urged from her seat.

The Firedrake was bearing down on them. Still Berrin couldn't get the light free. Frustrated, he felt like smashing it loose with his sword. He looked up to check the progress of the Firedrake and suddenly decided that any violent movements might not be such a good idea. The monster was already there, only ten metres away. It had stopped and was eyeing them warily.

'Olanda,' Berrin whispered. 'Don't move.'

Motionless and terrified, he stared at the strange creature. It was a sort of worm. No, a centipede, he decided when he saw the hundreds of legs beneath its long body. Its head was nothing like a centipede's though. He should have expected that from a monster created by Malig Tumora. This looked more like a cow. It even had horns protruding from its head. Worm, centipede, cow — whatever it was, it filled the tunnel.

Berrin added snake to his list when the Firedrake's lips parted and out poked a forked tongue. All the more reason to stand completely still. What was that at its tip? Each branch of the forked tongue was coiled around something. Fascinated despite his fear, his eyes locked onto them. They were round, hard, about the size of a bunched fist. Stones, he realised. Why would any creature bother to carry two stones in its mouth?

Then came the smell. Was there anything as putrid in the entire universe? The Firedrake opened its mouth and belched a foul breath from deep in its guts.

'Ugh, that's disgusting,' said Olanda. 'What kind of animal farts through its mouth?'

Berrin's eyes watered at the stink but he kept them on the Firedrake. There was something they were missing here. He watched as the Firedrake's tongue began to lash up and down and from side to side. Suddenly, it wrenched its tongue backwards and the forked tips jerked, giving out a sharp crack. The stones, thought Berrin. It's trying to do something with those stones.

'Why has it stopped back there?' he asked Olanda. 'It could move closer and crush us easily. Chew us up if it wants to.'

'Maybe it doesn't like raw food,' said Olanda with her hand to her nose.

The lashing had started once more. The Firedrake was going to perform that odd cracking of its tongue again. Berrin watched, mesmerised. It's as if it's trying to smash those two stones together in just the right way, he thought.

That was it!

His leg moved even before his mind had worked out what was happening. Using his foot as a paddle, he scooped water into the monster's face, desperately hoping it would be enough to save them. He saw the spray of water floating through the air and a little splashed onto the stones just as they crashed together.

The foul breath was a kind of gas — Berrin was sure of that now. One spark from those stones and the tunnel would become an inferno.

He scooped up more water, this time with his hands, drenching the Firedrake. The monster looked hurt that its meal was being so uncooperative.

'Berrin!' Olanda called.

'I'm coming!' he yelled. One more scoop of water should do it.

'Berrin! Can you hear anything?'

He turned around. The light of the Dodgem was aimed in the wrong direction and their helmet lamps were good for only a few metres, but he didn't need to see what was making that clicking sound. They'd all come to recognise it in the last few hours.

Somewhere ahead in the darkened tunnel, the scorpion was waiting for them.

TWELVE
Battle by Sonar

'GET IN,' SNAPPED OLANDA.

'What are you going to do? The tunnel is blocked in both directions.'

'Just get in,' she repeated.

Berrin obeyed, then turned to look at the Firedrake again. It was shaking the water from its tongue and funnelling its hot breath onto the stones. Any moment now, they would be dry. It belched a new cloud of that stinking gas, getting ready to fry them where they sat in the Dodgem.

Olanda slammed the lever forward just in time. A sheet of searing flame followed them as they accelerated along the tunnel towards the scorpion. The heat singed the hair on the back of Berrin's head. Fortunately, the gas was quickly consumed and the flame died as suddenly as it had begun.

The tunnel ahead of them went dark. Well, almost. The Dodgem's headlight was facing behind them and only a small part of its light was reflected back in their direction. They might as well have closed their eyes.

'What are you going to do?' Berrin shouted again. Surely she wasn't planning to ram the scorpion. It would blow them to pieces before they could get close enough. They were sitting ducks.

Olanda pressed down even harder on the lever. No time for explanations. 'Hold on!' she cried. They were in her hands now and she needed all of her concentration.

Berrin gripped the side of his seat and waited for the blast. Then he realised they were rising higher on the curved wall of the pipe. He had felt this odd sensation in his stomach only once before. Quinn had been the driver then. As he had that day, he let out a scream of fear and exhilaration as up they went, higher and higher, until they were upside down for just a brief instant.

It was as they started down the other side, hurtling along the pipe, defying gravity, that the scorpion fired its cannon. The missile flew harmlessly down the centre of the pipe. Harmless for the two Rats, that is. For the unfortunate Firedrake, it proved fatal as the monster of Sector Nine exploded in a fireball fed by its own foul gases.

OLANDA'S DARING TRICK WITH the Dodgem had won them a reprieve, but now they had to escape. There was no time to stop and try again to change the light. While they were still moving at breakneck speed, Berrin was finally able to loosen the headlight from behind him and hold it up above Olanda's head. His hands burned and his arms ached, but at least they could see the pipe ahead.

They sped on, turning down any tunnel that offered a straight run. Anything to keep a good distance between them and the scorpion.

Then the Dodgem stopped.

'The batteries have finally died,' said Berrin.

They crawled out and continued on foot. At any moment they expected an explosion. The scorpion would find the disabled Dodgem and blow it to pieces. Then it would come after them.

But the explosion never came.

'Maybe it didn't follow us,' Olanda suggested.

'I didn't actually see it chasing us from Sector Nine,' said Berrin.

'Where is it then?'

'It's a machine. It follows the orders it's been given. If it's not chasing us, then it has probably gone back to mapping the rest of the tunnels,' said Berrin with a rising sense of panic. 'It's gone back to where it left off.'

'Ferdinand,' whispered Olanda. 'It will blast away that access hole cover and ...'

Berrin had already started running. She left the rest of her sentence there in the tunnel and ran after him.

BERRIN AND OLANDA RAN, crawled through narrower pipes where they had to, then ran again. They were heading towards the base, though it was not their destination. The base would be no more than a charred ruin by now.

At last they reached the tunnel where Belle had led the others earlier.

'Where are they?' asked Olanda, puffing heavily.

'Not far away,' Berrin answered. 'Listen. There are voices.'

Olanda forced herself to breathe more quietly until she heard them too. In the silence, they strained their ears for the ominous clicks of the scorpion. Nothing. After five seconds, they relaxed and dared to smile at each other.

'This way,' said Berrin, pointing into a smaller pipe. 'Let's join the others.'

Two minutes later, they emerged into a chamber where they could stand up again. The Rats were there, most of them anyway. There was Dorian and Wendell and they had managed to get Belle through the pipe as well.

Everyone was pleased to see Berrin and Olanda back safely.

'We lured the scorpion away for a while but it's loose again,' reported Berrin.

'We know,' said Dorian. 'Belle's been following it. It's searching the tunnels again in a pattern. How far away now, Belle?' she asked.

'A few minutes,' the probe said, with a tremor of fear in her voice.

Berrin looked around the larger tunnel. They had parked the last Dodgem in the middle and stacked whatever they could salvage from the base on either side.

'A barricade!' he said. 'But the scorpion will blow it away with just a couple of shots.'

'It's the best we can do. It will take a little while to break through and we're going to use those seconds to attack it,' Dorian explained.

Some of the Rats had already drawn their swords.

Berrin's heart sank. What use were swords against the toughened shell of the scorpion? They wouldn't get close enough to lay steel on it anyway. It was a desperately heroic plan, but it would see them all killed.

'How long now, Belle?' Wendell asked. He had certainly changed his tune. Once, he had wanted her dead. Now he called her gently by name.

Belle put her hand to the wall, but dropped it almost immediately. Instead, she walked awkwardly to the barricade and, facing into the darkness of the tunnel, sent out a series of high-pitched clicks.

Sonar, thought Berrin. The same way that the scorpion itself navigated in the tunnels. He almost smiled that enemy and friend alike should make these strange clicks.

'It's here,' Belle announced.

Dorian reached into the Dodgem and switched on the headlight. There was the scorpion, dropped to its legs now and moving steadily towards them. Already, it was raising its tail and taking aim.

Berrin heard Belle send out a new series of clicks, as though the light wasn't enough for her. He didn't take his eyes from the scorpion. If he had, he might have missed its brief hesitation. At the moment Belle emitted those odd clicks, the scorpion veered just a few centimetres to the side. At the same time, its tail drooped.

As soon as Belle stopped, the robot was back on course and ready to blow them out of the tunnels forever.

'Do it again!' he urged Belle.

'Do what?' she asked politely.

'That sound you make. The clicking. Quickly, do it again.'

She seemed confused, but Berrin's orders were clear enough. She pointed her snout towards the scorpion and released a stronger series of clicks. There was no doubt about it. Those clicks were affecting the scorpion. This time it stopped and turned its entire body to one side.

Berrin didn't wait another second. He leaped onto the barricade and down the other side.

'Berrin, you'll be killed!' Olanda screamed.

Weren't they all about to die anyway? Wendell scrambled over the barricade as well. Both he and Berrin drew their swords and raced towards the enemy.

The scorpion's sonar might have been a little confused, but its heat sensors still worked. At this distance, two sweating human bodies were easily detected. It turned to face them and brought its tail-cannon into a steady firing position.

But before it could shoot, the tail started to wobble and tilt in odd directions as Belle bombarded it with clicks. Wendell and Berrin were only a few metres away when it fired.

The deafening explosion blew both boys off their feet. They were only dazed, however. The cannon had blown a hole in the concrete above their heads. Pebbles and powdered cement rained down on them as they lay before the scorpion.

They struggled to their feet, swords still in hand, and began to hammer against the enemy. It didn't back away. It didn't need to. The armoured plates covering its body deflected their blows easily. There was nothing they could do to hurt it.

Swinging its heavy tail like a club, the scorpion struck out at its attackers. First Wendell went down, then Berrin, left to face it alone, felt the smack of its hard steel against his hip. He was knocked off his feet and lay bruised and panting at the scorpion's mercy. His legs wouldn't respond. The best he could do was crawl backwards pathetically. Was there any point in even trying? He looked up to see the scorpion slowly lowering its tail into position. Any second now it would fire. There would not be enough of his body left to bury.

He lay there, waiting to die. The first explosion was still ringing in his ears, otherwise he might have heard the furious clicking noises that now filled the tunnel. Certainly, the scorpion could hear them. It turned its aim away from the two helpless boys. Without warning, it veered right around and rolled a little way into the darkness. Then it spun quickly again and returned, menacingly.

Its tail swayed and jerked above its body. Suddenly, it fired off a shot, but this one flew in the opposite direction, the explosion lighting the tunnel briefly.

Now the scorpion began a frenzied dance, spinning, lashing its tail like a whip. On the ground, Berrin was recovering quickly and Wendell too. They backed away towards the barricade, their eyes glued to the scorpion's tail. Its next shot could go anywhere.

The scorpion seemed to regain a little control and remembered the two humans who had attacked it. It turned towards them and lowered its tail until it aimed straight at them. But the tail kept moving, arching further and further forward. When it had dipped as far as it could go, it fired.

The tunnel filled with flames and dust and the dreadful sound of steel ripping as easily as a tattered shirt. Behind the barricade, the Rats were thrown to the ground by the blast. Before it, poor Berrin and Wendell were scorched and peppered by debris. But they were alive and mostly unhurt.

At last the dust settled and an eerie silence replaced the fading echoes. Berrin dared to look for the robot. When he found it, he saw that the deadly machine would hunt them no more. With its final shot, the scorpion had blown itself to pieces.

THIRTEEN
The Scorpion's Tail

BERRIN BRUSHED FRAGMENTS OF concrete from his hair and dust from his clothes. While he felt himself for broken bones or gashes oozing blood, his eyes stayed on the scorpion. Tangled wires bulged out from between the twisted plates of steel. Those heat-seeking 'eyes' were gone altogether. One thing remained intact. Still arched over that ravaged body was the weapon that had destroyed it, the cannon hidden within its own tail.

'Careful, it might explode,' Olanda warned when Berrin edged towards it.

No, he decided. It can't harm us now. He reached down and touched the tail. It was still hot from firing but not hot enough to burn him. He grasped it firmly near the base, where it was attached to the damaged body. To his surprise, it broke off and he found himself nursing the weapon in his hands.

'Hey, watch where you're pointing that thing,' called Wendell. He hadn't come forward to inspect the carcass with the rest. Instead, he had climbed back over the barricade. Berrin looked up to see him stooped over Belle who had collapsed onto the ground.

Gently, Wendell lifted her head. After a moment or two, she opened her eyes. 'I'm sorry,' she said. 'It's the noise, you see.' With senses as highly tuned as hers, the explosions had left her dazed and grimacing in pain.

'You saved us,' Wendell said. 'Your sonar confused the scorpion. Without you, it would have blown *us* to pieces instead of itself.'

The rest of the Rats were on their feet, shaking dust from their hair and daring to hope they would survive another day. They gathered round Belle, who was sitting up now. 'Thank you, Belle,' they muttered, one by one. All except

Berrin and Olanda, who continued to inspect the scorpion's tail.

'Be careful you don't fire that thing,' growled Wendell.

Until this warning, Berrin hadn't thought about trying to use the cannon. He stared down at the weapon in his hands. 'Do you think I could?' he asked Olanda.

She shrugged. 'Is there a trigger, like the crossbow has?'

But of course there wasn't. The cannon had been part of the scorpion's body, firing on command from its thinking circuits.

'Too bad we can't use it against the Gadges,' said Olanda.

'Yeah, too bad,' Berrin agreed in a vague murmur. He didn't put it down though. There was something about the weight of it in his hands and the sight all around him of what it could do . . .

Dorian soon had him thinking about other things. 'Food,' she said, and that one word suddenly reminded them all of their hunger. 'The scorpion destroyed our supplies. We must find more, and quickly.'

She sent four Rats off to scavenge what they could. 'Ruben, Vindy, you try again with the electricity. If we can't recharge our batteries soon, we might as well have let the scorpion finish us off.'

She seemed to be saving Berrin and Olanda until last. 'This Dodgem is the only one still working,' she said, nodding towards the steel frame buried beneath the barricade. 'You two will need it. I have a special job for you.'

THE SPECIAL JOB WAS A mission to the surface. 'Ferdinand wants to know if our last adventure made any difference,' Dorian explained.

'Cutting that pipe, you mean?'

'Yes. Go back to the same part of the city and take a look. Find out whether the Gadges realise what we did. Are the grown-ups acting strangely? That sort of thing.'

The pair found themselves on the move yet again. 'I'm driving,' Berrin announced.

Olanda laughed as she climbed into the rear seat. 'You're afraid I'll try the upside-down trick again, aren't you?'

'Yes,' he answered bluntly.

'Coward.'

'At least I'm not crazy.'

They swapped insults as they travelled along. It helped to keep fear at bay. If the Gadges had found the break in the pipe, they might have set up an ambush, expecting the Rats to return.

They were especially careful when they emerged from the hidden access hole. It was a relief when they spotted the first Gadge.

'If they're out and about, then there's no ambush,' Berrin whispered.

They crept from bush to bush and under low-hanging trees. 'Careful of the wind,' Olanda warned. They couldn't allow their scent to drift into the nose of a Gadge.

They found the broken pipe. At least, they found the place where Wendell had cut it in two. It was being fixed as they watched, unseen, from a hundred metres away. Gadger Red himself stood over two of his companions as they worked.

Berrin and Olanda didn't dare go any closer. There were more Gadges roaming the streets than they had ever seen before.

'Do you think they know about the scorpion already?' Olanda said.

Berrin shook his head. 'No, not yet. It's only been an hour or two.'

'Then why so many Gadges in this part of the city?'

As Berrin and Olanda watched from their hideaway, two came galloping by on all fours. One carried a small cylinder tied around his neck. Moments later they were back and Olanda had an answer to her question. The Gadges weren't hunting Rats, they were after grown-ups.

'You can't do this!' cried a human voice. 'Let me go. I won't live like a prisoner any more.'

They peeped between the thick branches of a tree to see the Gadges, on their hind legs now, marching a grown-up along between them. One of them tried to press a mask over the grown-up's face. The man turned and twisted until the second Gadge grabbed his hair roughly and held him still. Now the mask was in place, drawing gas through a thin tube from the cylinder. Instantly, the grown-up stopped fighting and by the time they were out of sight, he was walking without a fuss.

'Did you see his eyes?' Olanda asked Berrin when they were gone.

'Yes,' he answered eagerly. 'Before they put the mask on him, there was a real spark in them, to show how alive he was inside.'

Like yours, he thought, grinning at his friend. He didn't know it, but Olanda was thinking exactly the same thing about him.

They had seen enough. Besides, Olanda's stomach was growling loud enough for the Gadges to hear. They slipped unnoticed through the same access hole and sped towards base.

Dorian was waiting for them. 'I had to keep these back from the others,' she said, passing a bread roll to each of them. The rolls were still warm. Their aroma wafted through the pipe, drawing the eyes of the others. 'Don't worry about them,' Dorian laughed. 'They've had their share.' A few Rats moaned in protest.

'What about those?' asked Olanda when she saw two more rolls in a sack hanging from Dorian's arm.

'For Ferdinand. He'll be hungrier than anyone. Come on, Berrin, you'll need to tell him what you saw on the surface.'

'Take the scorpion's tail with you, Berrin,'

Olanda urged him. 'Maybe Ferdinand can work out a way to make it fire.'

FERDINAND'S TUNNEL WAS dark when Dorian led Berrin through the final opening.

'I'm here,' called a voice. 'The battery on the helmet you gave me died a few hours ago.'

They had no spare to give him. For now, they sat in a circle using only Dorian's helmet lamp. Ferdinand ate the first of his rolls slowly, tearing off pieces a little at a time.

Isn't he hungry, Berrin wondered. If he doesn't want the second roll, I'll gladly eat it for him. Then he felt ashamed. Couldn't he see that Ferdinand wasn't well? The human body wasn't made to be locked up in a dark and stuffy space like this.

Ferdinand's cheeks glowed a little, though, when Berrin described what he had seen on the surface. 'It's true then. The gas is what makes them obey Malig Tumora. Without the smell of those flowers, the blind obedience disappears.'

He peppered Berrin with more questions. Mostly, the boy had no answer. There was so much more they had to know. But for now, it seemed they should celebrate.

'We have a definite aim now, Dorian,' Ferdinand said. 'If we can't destroy the flowers that make the gas, perhaps we can cut the pipes that carry it to the buildings where the grown-ups live and work. Malig Tumora is vulnerable. We can defeat him.'

Dorian was eager to get back to base. On their last visit, with the scorpion rampaging through the tunnels, it had seemed Malig Tumora would soon defeat them. Now there was hope.

Berrin had put the scorpion's tail aside when they first arrived. Moving quickly to join Dorian, he would have forgotten it altogether if Ferdinand hadn't called out to him. Inspecting it more closely, Ferdinand guessed what it was.

'I can't work out how to fire it,' Berrin told him.

Ferdinand signalled Dorian to shine her helmet lamp on the oddly curved steel. He flexed it until the tail was almost straight, then bent it back into a semi-circle as far as it would go. There were no wires dangling from the broken end, just a thick web of matted threads.

'See these,' he said, flicking the threads. 'They're not for carrying electrical signals. If I know Malig Tumora, he will have devised something special.'

'It's too dangerous to experiment with,' said Dorian, eyeing the scorpion's tail suspiciously. 'Leave it here, Berrin.'

Berrin was reluctant to obey her, but at the same time he knew she was right. If he tinkered with it, he might blow himself up, just as the scorpion had done. The explosion might kill a handful of his friends too. It wasn't worth the risk.

Then something happened that made him forget the scorpion's tail altogether. The dark light bulb above their heads suddenly filled Ferdinand's home with its golden glow.

FOURTEEN
A Trickle of Water

LIFE WAS LOOKING UP for the Doomsday Rats. The scorpion had been destroyed. They had electric power again for their lights and their battery chargers. Better still, one of the scavenging parties had brought back a feast, as Dorian and Berrin discovered when they returned to base.

'What's that fabulous smell?' Berrin asked as he crawled into the sleeping chamber.

The other Rats were sitting impatiently amid the ruins of their hammocks and other supplies. Every mouth was watering. Every eye was turned towards Quinn.

'It's a chicken,' Quinn announced as Berrin and Dorian took their places.

'A roast chicken,' someone breathed.

It didn't look much like a chicken at that moment, Berrin thought. The head and legs were gone, the feathers too. All he could see was golden-brown skin and pale pink flesh as Quinn tore the chicken to pieces with his hands.

'Where did you get it?'

'I stole it from the Gadges,' said Quinn proudly.

From the Gadges! That was brave indeed. The others were almost as eager to hear his story as they were to receive their piece of the chicken.

'They were roasting it over an open fire, you see. I could smell it.' Quinn paused to make sure they were hanging on his every word. 'I crept up close, but they were too busy with the chicken to keep watch. Then I threw some stones into the trees to cause a distraction. They all trooped off to investigate and that was when I . . .'

'Liar,' said Olanda with a laugh of contempt. 'I was there too, Quinn. Tell them what really happened.'

Quinn looked caught out and rather reluctant to stick with the truth. Olanda stared him down.

'Oh, all right. Olanda and I smelled the chicken roasting from down in the pipes. We crept out carefully and saw three Gadges standing around the fire.'

He enjoyed having their attention and looked ready to exaggerate the story all over again. One heated glance from Olanda was enough to put him back on track.

'Then Gadger Red came along. He barked an order at them. We didn't hear it, but the other Gadges didn't look too impressed. They argued with him, pointing at the chicken. But Gadger Red wouldn't listen. He sent them off to do some job or other before they could even take a bite.'

Olanda finished the story for him. 'Once they were gone, we walked in and took it.'

As for the chicken, the Rats all finished it together.

It was getting late by then. With a full belly for the first time in days, most of the children simply lay down on the cold concrete and went to sleep. Berrin was preparing to do the same when he heard whispering. He looked about the dimly lit chaos of the sleeping chamber to find the source. Belle was speaking to Dorian.

'Are you sure?' he heard Dorian ask.

Others had heard them too. 'What is it? Can you hear something, Belle?'

She nodded unhappily. 'It's coming from the entrance to the tunnels, I think.'

'The Gadges are coming back. Is that it?'

Many of the Rats were sitting up again, all thought of sleep chased away.

'No, it's not the Gadges. At least, I'm sure they're not searching the pipes again. There are no footsteps, no voices.'

'Then what can you hear?'

She fell silent for a long time. She didn't mean it, but this hesitation left the others more worried than ever. 'It's an odd kind of echo, really. Almost as though ... yes, it sounds like the opening to one of the large pipes is being closed off.'

'Quinn, take the Dodgem and see if you can find out what's happening,' Dorian ordered.

While they waited for him to return, Dorian spoke again to Belle. She wasn't doing well down in the pipes, Berrin noticed. If they hadn't insisted, she would have left her share of the precious chicken uneaten. Now she spoke again, whispering to Dorian who then passed on the news.

'There's something else,' she explained to the anxious Rats. 'Belle can feel some intense heat up on the surface. It's happening all over the place, at twenty or thirty spots.'

'Intense heat,' Wendell repeated. 'What does that mean?'

Belle was concentrating too hard to respond. Her thick purple tongue tasted the air, her ears twitched. She held her huge hands open before her, fingers spread wide to expose the bat-like webbing between them. 'Access holes,' she said at last.

This made little sense at first. They floundered in confusion, each Rat offering a separate explanation. Then Wendell spoke up. 'Ferdinand told me once how the Dodgems were made, in the Time Before. The steel is burned under a special flame until it is red hot. Then it can be moulded and stuck together. It's called welding.'

'You think the Gadges are doing this welding to the access holes? What good will that do them?' Berrin asked.

'Maybe it's not really the access holes,' said Dorian in a tone that unsettled them all. 'What if they are welding the steel covers into place?'

'So they can't be opened, you mean?' asked Berrin.

The sound of a Dodgem in the large pipe outside disturbed them. Moments later, Quinn crawled in, breathless and excited. 'Belle was right,' he announced immediately. 'They're sealing up the openings to the big pipes. Not just one. All of them.'

The Doomsday Rats were left to guess what was going on. Most settled on Dorian's idea. 'Malig Tumora is scared of us. He's worried we'll sneak out and sabotage his pipelines again so he's trying to keep us down here, out of the way.'

They stretched out to sleep again. Tomorrow they would work out what to do. For now, with the openings to the tunnel system closed up, they were safer than they had ever been. At least, that was how it seemed.

LONG AFTER THE OTHERS SLEPT, Belle kept listening. It was Wendell, once her enemy, who stayed awake beside her. Finally, he saw her face change and knew that she had heard something.

Strangely, he could hear it too. It was the sound every Rat disliked: the trickle of water that meant it was raining on the surface. This was the price you paid if you lived in storm-water pipes. When it rained, the water invaded your home.

But Wendell soon realised this was different. 'Dorian!' he called and shook the girl awake.

Berrin was close by and sat up at the same time as their leader. 'What is it?' he asked.

'Water,' whispered Wendell.

'So it's raining on the surface,' said Dorian, still half asleep and not very pleased to be woken up.

'No, listen,' Wendell insisted.

Berrin was already doing just that. Water, yes, but this was no trickle. It was gushing into the tunnels a long way off.

Belle confirmed it. 'In five places,' she said. 'Through some kind of tube. The Gadges have pushed huge tubes into the only access holes still open. I can feel the vibration. They are pumping water into the tunnels.'

'What for?' Berrin asked.

It was Dorian who answered. 'Malig Tumora

has a new plan. He's flooding the tunnels. He's going to drown us all.'

OVER THE NEXT HOUR, THE high hopes the Rats had enjoyed turned to despair. All the large pipes that opened into rivers and lakes had been closed off. Most of the access holes were sealed, and those that weren't were heavily guarded.

Olanda had discovered this in a most painful way. Finding an access hole cover that she could budge, she pushed it up, only to have a Gadge slash at her hand with his vicious claws. Now she sat in the corner of the sleeping chamber with a blood-soaked bandage tied tightly around her wrist.

The rest sat glumly nearby. At that moment, it truly did seem that they were the Doomsday Rats.

'There must be an opening that they haven't found,' Quinn insisted.

Maybe there was, but the tunnels were filling with water so quickly that it was already difficult to get around. Besides, there was one terrible thought that tormented them all. Even if they could find a safe way out of the tunnels for themselves, Ferdinand was trapped.

Dorian had already been down to see him. 'He wants us all to escape, however we can. He insists.'

'But he'll drown. Can't we do something?' said Berrin.

Dorian shook her head silently. Ferdinand had not been able to offer her any ideas. As their leader, she felt powerless. The sound of water filling the pipes grew louder by the minute.

'I'm going down to be with Ferdinand,' she told them.

The tone of her voice hinted at something else. She was not coming back.

'I'll come too,' said Vindy, and before they knew it, Quinn was on the move as well and many more with him.

Berrin looked across at Olanda. Her face was drained of colour. She looked like Ferdinand when they had first seen him, a ghost. 'Should we go with them?' she asked.

'It seems like giving up,' he answered, but he could see that Olanda wanted to be with the others.

There were only two other Rats left at the base with them now. Wendell and Belle were too big to crawl through the narrow tunnels leading to Ferdinand's home. They followed Berrin and Olanda anyway, as far as the large pipe where the scorpion had been destroyed. Its broken shell lay there still and without its tail it was hard to remember why they had feared it so much.

'We'll wait here,' said Wendell.

Wait for what, Berrin wondered. For the other Rats to return or for the flood waters to drown them?

Wendell's helmet lamp had died. Berrin took off his own and handed it to the boy who had rescued him and brought him to these tunnels. Then, by the light of Olanda's lamp alone, he helped his injured friend crawl down to Ferdinand's grim prison where they would all die.

FIFTEEN

Darkness and Death

THE DEEP GASH ACROSS Olanda's hand made crawling through the narrow pipes slow and painful. She was exhausted when they arrived. Dorian helped her find a space on the floor to rest. It wasn't easy. Ferdinand's home was never intended to house all his Rats.

'Berrin, you've come as well,' Ferdinand said when he saw his nephew emerge from the pipe behind Olanda. He didn't seem very pleased.

'I can't bear to think of you down here alone,' Berrin responded.

'But I'm not alone, am I? Help me persuade them.' Ferdinand turned to the others, sweeping a hand across the scene in frustration. 'If you stay here with me, you will all die,' he said to them. 'It's a terrible waste. You should be searching for a way out of the tunnels.'

'Not without you. We can't abandon you,' said Quinn.

'But you must. You can't save me, but you can save yourselves. You must fight on. We know what to do now. The pipes that carry the flower gas to the houses and the buildings where the grown-ups work — if you can destroy them faster than Malig Tumora can repair them, we have a chance.'

None of the dispirited children would raise their faces to look at him. None but Berrin.

Ferdinand saw that solitary face and appealed to him. 'Escape, Berrin, please, for my sake. If anyone can find a way out of the tunnels it's you. Stay alive today and you can take up the struggle again tomorrow.'

Berrin stared around the cramped tunnel. These were the bravest people he had ever known. Now, they had decided to use up the last of their courage by dying here with Ferdinand. He couldn't get angry at them, as Ferdinand seemed to be. After all, their chance at victory had vanished. At least staying together like this until the end was a kind of victory.

'I want to stay,' he said.

Ferdinand grimaced and began to cough. 'No, no,' he moaned between bitter jerks of his wasted frame. 'This is not how it should end.'

Berrin had made up his mind. There was nothing Ferdinand could say to him that would change it. Or so he thought.

The sound of rushing water grew louder. How long before it began to pour into this part of the system? How long would it take to fill the space where they all huddled, covering their ankles first, then their knees, their waists, chests and finally . . .

'Are you going to let Malig Tumora win after all?' Ferdinand asked him. 'Will you give up on the Time Before? It was a good life, and the world was a great place to live, before Malig Tumora turned his powers against us. We can have it back again, as long as we don't give up. You most of all, Berrin. My brother is up there, your father, and your mother too. They would remember the Time Before, if only they could get the chance. It's up to you to give them that chance.'

These words stunned Berrin like no others Ferdinand had uttered. He had forgotten about the Time Before and the grown-ups. Most of all, he had forgotten the sensations that sparked through his whole body whenever he thought of his parents. He had almost died struggling to free them. But that wasn't what he was doing here.

He couldn't look Ferdinand in the face. When he turned away, ashamed and confused, his eyes fell on the scorpion's tail lying in the dust where he had left it on his last visit. Ferdinand followed his eye and saw what he was staring at. His coughing fit had passed now and he snatched up the scorpion's tail and shoved it into Berrin's hands.

'Take this. I looked it over. Years ago, before I escaped into the tunnels, I saw fibres like that. They carried thought signals inside Malig Tumora's robots, like the nerves in a human body. If you hold them tightly and think of what you want the cannon to do there's a chance you can make it fire.'

He saw that Berrin's resolve was weakening. 'Go back into the tunnels, Berrin, before it's too late. Find a way out. Use this cannon to destroy the glasshouses.'

Berrin looked towards the others, Olanda most of all. Exhaustion and defeat had made her drift off to sleep. She couldn't help him this time, not with her hand so badly slashed. No-one else seemed ready to volunteer. There was only him.

Then the light bulb above their heads died. There wasn't a single helmet lamp still working. Darkness had arrived early and following soon in its footsteps would come a cold and watery death.

BERRIN STRUGGLED ALONG the narrow tunnel. The scorpion's tail was heavy and awkward to carry. He couldn't see even his own hand before his eyes, but at least he knew these pipes. What he would do without light once he left them, he had no idea.

Something crawled across his hand. He yelped and pulled it away only to hear the reproach of a familiar squeak. Jasper had come with him. He placed his hand down again and let the little creature climb onto his shoulder.

Soon after, he emerged from the smallest pipe into a straight-sided chamber. Now at least he could stretch out a bit. He took a breather, but as he leaned against the wall, his back touched something unexpected. It rolled away a few centimetres, scraping against the concrete as it went. The access hole cover. His companions had managed to steal it when they were trying to stop the scorpion and brought it here, hoping to seal off the entrance to Ferdinand's prison. Thankfully, the scorpion had never made it this far.

Berrin was about to move on when he froze in his place. Seal off the entrance ... Yes, that was it! What had Dorian said when she ordered the access hole cover brought here? *Even a few seconds could be precious.* It might buy more than a few seconds, he hoped.

Without any light, he could only feel with his hands. He rolled the access hole cover into place across the opening to the pipe and pressed it firmly into place. He felt around the perimeter with his fingers. The seal was almost perfect, and when the floodwater pressed its immense weight against the metal, it would become even tighter.

'They'll suffocate eventually, I suppose,' he said aloud to Jasper. 'That's if I don't find a way to rescue them.'

He crawled on, with Jasper clinging to his shoulder, until he saw a faint light ahead. Wendell and Belle. The helmet lamp he had given them was still working.

As he stood up in the large pipe and walked the last few metres to join them, water began to pool around his ankles.

'BERRIN,' WENDELL CALLED WHEN he recognised him. 'I thought you'd all gone to die alongside Ferdinand.'

'Change of plan. He convinced me to die out here instead.' Berrin looked down at Belle who didn't seem afraid at all.

'What's that in your hands?' she asked.

'The scorpion's tail. Ferdinand is hoping that I can —' He stopped. The bitter cold around his calves reminded him how quickly the water was rising. Who was he kidding? This pipe was where he would die, just as he had joked to Wendell. He had come close to dying here once already, he realised, as he saw the twisted remains of the scorpion disappearing beneath the water. It shifted in the current, knocking against the chunks of concrete that had fallen when it blew a hole in the tunnel above their heads.

Berrin looked up at that gaping hole. The bare earth was exposed and a rusting spike of steel reinforcement protruded from the broken concrete. He took Jasper from his shoulder and perched him on the spike. 'You will be the last of us to drown,' he said solemnly.

The water lapped at his knees. Already Belle was finding it hard to stay on her feet in the powerful current.

'Lean against me,' Wendell told her.

His strength kept her from slipping away, but before long it would take him as well and Berrin too. When the water reached the boys' waists, poor Belle had difficulty keeping her head above the surface.

Not long now, thought Berrin. He looked up to check on Jasper, but the jagged spur of steel was bare. He's gone then, Berrin said to himself. Slipped into the water. Perhaps he jumped to get it over with quickly.

Wendell struggled to keep Belle afloat. In his heart, Berrin could feel the last warmth of hope giving way to the chill of death.

'What's that he's got in his mouth?' Wendell asked suddenly.

'Who are you talking about?' Berrin said.

'That rat of yours. Look, there he is, above your head.'

Berrin looked up and, sure enough, in the weakening beam of Wendell's helmet lamp he saw Jasper. The little creature hadn't fallen into the water after all. And Wendell was right, he did have something in his mouth.

Berrin reached up and took whatever it was from that tiny jaw. 'Shine your light on it,' he called to Wendell.

There, he could see it clearly now. Something he had never thought to see down here in the darkened tunnels. Yet there it was and the sight of it rekindled the dying flame of hope.

It was a blade of grass.

SIXTEEN
A Choice of Targets

'GRASS!' BERRIN BREATHED IN amazement. 'And look, it's fresh and green.'

Both he and Wendell stared up at Jasper. Where could he have got such a thing, down here in the tunnels? Unfortunately, the little rat could not tell them. His kind were no fools, however, and he could see the waters rising higher. He seemed to decide it was time to save himself. As the two boys watched, he climbed from his perch of rusty steel into the hole blown by the scorpion's cannon.

'Hey, he's gone again,' said Wendell. They craned their necks, checking the hole in the concrete.

'There's only one place he could go. He's found a crack in the dirt above us!' Wendell cried. 'There is a way! A way up to the surface.'

'Shine your light onto it,' ordered Berrin. He was aware suddenly of the echo. The space left above the water was much smaller now and it altered the sound of their voices.

Wendell tilted his head back until they could see clearly where the earth had been blown away. There was the tiny opening where Jasper had disappeared.

'How far is it to the surface, do you think?'

'What does it matter?' Wendell replied. 'It's our only chance.' As he spoke, he groaned with the effort of keeping Belle above the water.

'Leave me,' she whispered. 'I'm just a weight to you now.'

They ignored her. Berrin was already stretching up onto his toes, clawing desperately at the dirt. It was hard and stony. His fingers were soon bleeding and yet he had barely made the hole any bigger. 'We'll never dig our way out like this.' To make matters worse, he could only use one hand. With the other, he clutched the scorpion's tail.

'Can you use that thing?' Wendell asked.

He thought Berrin might use it as a shovel to dig the dirt away. But to Berrin, the question meant something entirely different. What had Ferdinand said about the mass of threads? *Hold them tightly and think of what you want the cannon to do.* Would it work?

'Move up the tunnel,' he called to Wendell.

'But our only chance is this hole.'

'I know that,' he snapped and brandished the scorpion's tail. 'I'm going to blast it with this thing.'

'You're crazy.'

'Just do as I say!' Berrin shouted angrily. The water was already up to their waists.

He was about to move off when Jasper's whiskered snout appeared through the narrow opening.

'You've come back for me, have you? Well, you'd better come here,' Berrin called. Smiling briefly, he reached up and took the rat onto the back of his hand. 'Onto my shoulder. Go on.'

Jasper obeyed as Berrin waded against the current. A few metres was all he could manage. Now for the scorpion's tail.

He entwined his fingers in the filaments that dangled from one end of the cannon. The other end, the barrel, he aimed towards the broken concrete. Think! Think of what he wanted the cannon to do.

Nothing happened.

'Come on!' Wendell urged. 'There's not much time.'

Think! Berrin tried all sorts of things. He pictured what he wanted to happen. He commanded the cannon to fire. He pretended he was pulling a trigger in his mind. Nothing.

'That thing is useless. Go back to the hole and start digging again,' Wendell demanded.

Perhaps he was right. Berrin had done everything that Ferdinand had suggested and what use had it been? Soon, they would lose their chance to do anything at all. The water was above his navel.

'One last try,' he insisted.

To the robot, the cannon wasn't a separate weapon. It was its tail, a part of itself. Berrin set his eyes on the target again and, with his fingers gripped tightly on the mess of threads, he imagined the cannon was a part of him.

When he wanted his legs to walk, he didn't have to think about it. When he wanted his eyes to focus, he didn't have to control his muscles with his mind. It just happened. He stopped concentrating, stopped thinking, and instead felt for a connection directly into the scorpion's tail. *It's no different from my arms, my fingers. It's a part of me.*

At that moment, the cannon fired.

The noise was louder than anything he could have imagined. He blacked out for a second, but the bitter chill of the water brought him round before he collapsed.

For Belle, the noise was terrible. She screamed in agony and struggled in Wendell's grip. He did his best to soothe her as Berrin went to inspect the damage he had caused.

'It's working,' he cried gleefully. 'I've blown away a whole chunk. And look, I can see a tiny patch of light. We're almost through. I'm going to fire again, from here this time.'

'No!' Wendell shouted. 'It's too much for Belle.'

'Cover her ears then,' Berrin called back.

'What good will that do? She hears with her whole body. The pain must be terrible.'

What could Berrin do? This was their only chance, their last chance. He could blast a way for them to escape or they could die here in the rising waters. And it wasn't just his life. Ferdinand, Olanda, Dorian, Quinn — they were trapped with only an hour's air to breathe before they would die. There were the grown-ups to think about too. If he didn't free them from Malig Tumora's control, the struggle was over. No, he couldn't stop.

'Watch out!' he called, and seconds later he fired again.

Clods of dirt fell into the water around him. Some smacked into his face. But when the dust and smoke had cleared, the opening was wide enough for him to climb through to the surface. Sunlight had never looked so good.

'We've done it!' he cried in triumph.

Aiming carefully, he tossed the scorpion's tail up through the hole and into the open air. He had both hands free now. 'Here, Jasper, you can climb up yourself,' he said, setting the rodent on its way. Then he hauled himself up and out of the water.

Immediately, he turned around awkwardly until he was almost upside down. 'Bring Belle,' he called to Wendell. 'We'll get her out first.'

But when Wendell came into view beneath him, the light from above spilling brightly onto his face, Berrin gasped. Belle was floating on her back, with her eyes closed.

'It was too much for her,' Wendell explained.

For a horrible moment, Berrin feared she was dead. Then her eyes flicked open and she flailed her arms desperately. She was still alive.

He reached down for her, doing his best to get a hold. It wasn't easy. He had little to hold onto himself and the water dripping from his body made the dirt of the hole slippery.

Somehow, with Berrin pulling and Wendell pushing from below, they raised Belle out of the water. But Wendell was right. The ordeal was simply too much for a creature like Belle. Hanging halfway in and halfway out of the tunnel, she fainted again. Her body slumped heavily in the boys' uncertain grip. Before they could grab another hold, she slipped into the water again and was swept away by the greedy current.

'Belle!' Wendell cried. It was all he could do to hold himself in place.

Berrin reached down, offering his muddy arm. 'I've got you, Wendell!' he shouted, as the boy took hold. The grip was firm, Berrin's body now jammed securely into the hole he had blasted. In seconds, he would have him safely out of the water.

'She saved us, Berrin. She beat the scorpion for us. I can't let her drown like this.'

'No!' Berrin cried. 'She's gone, Wendell. There's nothing you can do for her.'

Wendell looked into Berrin's face. 'I've got to try,' he said calmly and then he let go.

'Wendell! Wendell!' Berrin shouted, but there was no answer. He knew in his heart that no-one could fight that surging water. If he fell in now, he was finished as well. Cautiously, he turned in the slippery hole to face the sunlight. 'I'm the only one left,' he muttered miserably. 'I am the last chance.'

He worked his way higher until he was through the ragged opening and flopped, exhausted, onto the grass.

Where was Jasper? No sign of him, but the scorpion's tail was there. He snatched it up. After weeks underground, he was uncomfortable in the open. Even the sun on his pale skin didn't make him feel any better.

Worse still, the Gadges might have heard the explosions as he blasted his way free of the tunnel. He'd better be gone before they came to investigate.

But where was he going? He had a powerful weapon in his hands and he had discovered how to fire it. But what should be his target? He thought of Ferdinand's final, desperate plea. The glasshouses.

He couldn't think of Ferdinand without seeing his friends scattered around their leader, waiting to die.

He had to choose. He had to choose now!

THERE WERE GADGES EVERYWHERE, in the streets, on the roofs of tall buildings. He couldn't afford to be caught. He was the last hope.

This thought weighed him down. Didn't he have enough to worry about, just staying free? He pushed it to the back of his mind. Concentrate, he told himself. Find the first target. Destroy it. Think of nothing else.

It took him longer than he'd hoped to find it, but he was in place now. He had a clear view of the target. He felt the scorpion's tail in his hands and hoped he could still make it fire.

He paused for a moment. Once he fired off this first shot, they would be after him. He hoped to destroy more sites like this, but they would surely stop him sooner or later. Had he chosen the right target?

Yes, he told himself. There had never been any other choice.

He raised the scorpion's tail, lined up the barrel with his eye and once again let it become part of him. It took a little longer this time, but finally the cannon jerked in his hands and he saw the missile in flight.

The explosion ripped through the silent morning. Perfect. He had hit the target just where he'd wanted to. Plumes of water shot into the air. There was a whooshing noise, like the belch of an enormous monster.

Water, unstoppable water, more powerful than anything Berrin had ever seen, began to surge below him. He should be on the move, find another target like this, but he couldn't help himself. He stood there for a few seconds more, watching it.

Berrin had not destroyed a glasshouse, as Ferdinand had insisted. He had blown open one of the storm-water pipes blocked off by Malig Tumora. In the minutes that followed, he used the scorpion's tail to blow open many more. The creeks and rivers were quickly awash with the escaping water. Inside the tunnels, the water level would be falling quickly. He hoped it would have dropped away from the access hole cover by now and his friends could crawl free.

It was then that the first of the Gadges spotted him. He ducked out of sight quickly, but it was only a matter of time. Perhaps he could get off one more shot, open one more of the blocked pipes.

He scrambled along the bank of a creek already swollen with floodwaters. There were two Gadges after him now, or was it three? They had already fired at him once. He had fired back, making them duck for cover and earning another minute or two of freedom.

Then he stopped dead in his tracks. It wasn't the Gadges that made him halt. No, he had glimpsed something in the fast-flowing water . . . a fox-like head and a large hand with black webbing between the fingers.

It was Belle, floating on her back, her eyes closed, as they had been in the tunnel less than an hour before. But this time there was no doubt. Belle was dead. She had been the last of her kind. They were all gone now.

Bobbing lifelessly beside her was a human body. It lay face down in the water, but Berrin knew all too well that it was Wendell.

With that sad sight before his weary eyes, Berrin forgot where he was and what he had set himself to do. The scorpion's tail hung uselessly at his side. It was in those few moments, when he let his guard down, that the Gadges rushed him from behind.

Before he realised what had happened, he was their prisoner.

James Moloney lives in Brisbane with his wife and three children. He has worked as an art union ticket seller, a gopher at a wholesale fruit market and a teacher.

These days he devotes most of his time to what he loves best — writing books for young people, two of which have won the Australian Children's Book of the Year Award: *Swashbuckler* in 1996 and *A Bridge to Wiseman's Cove* in 1997. His comic novel for young adults, *Black Taxi*, was shortlisted for the 2004 Adelaide Festival Children's Literature Award and the 2004 Children's Book Council Award for Older Readers.

It was a beast Berrin feared even more than another that saved him that day. As the Gadges were slicing him up with their eyes, Gadger Red appeared around a corner. Berrin had seen him once before. From that day, he had hoped never to be this close again.

'I'll take this boy,' he growled.

Alone, Berrin is captured by the Gadges and they are keen to eat him alive. But Malig Tumora has plans for Berrin that will make such a grizzly fate seem welcome. Behind high walls and amid blood-curdling squeals and roars, Berrin finds himself imprisoned in Malig Tumora's menagerie – a store house of the madman's failed experiments – and the sight of a new experiment that may change the future of mankind forever.

The Tunnels of Ferdinand
The Doomsday Rats Book One
James Moloney

The Doomsday Rats: Book One

The Tunnels of Ferdinand

A city under a spell and the children are the only ones who can free it.

All his life. Berrin has lived in a dormitory with hundreds of other children, guarded by the inhuman Dfx.

Then one day he is rescued by the Rats, a resistance group of children who secretly survive in the storm-water tunnels beneath the city. He learns that the city is controlled by the evil Malig Tumora and policed by his fearsome creations — including the monstrous Gadges and their leader, Gadger Red.

The only one who remembers what life was like before Malig Tumora took over is Ferdinand, the founder of the Rats. But he has grown too big for the tunnels and is in hiding outside the city — or is he?

Soon Berrin will not only discover the truth about Ferdinand, but he will also find that he himself holds the key to defeating Malig Tumora and saving the city . . .